"You wanted to be kissed, my lady. See where it got you?"

Thorne set Kit down gently, still half supporting her. "That's all there is to it, by the way. I'm quite a bit older and I'm very strong-minded."

"So am I," Kit protested.

"But we're not like-minded. My intention is to befriend you, not play out an extreme fantasy. You're very beautiful and you're becoming aware of your own power, but you can't cut your eyeteeth on me. That would be difficult and dangerous."

"You *do* take yourself seriously!"

"Forgive me—I'm not into exploiting young girls. I'm at war with myself even now for kissing you. Stay in love with love for a while, Christy. Adult love has a ruthless side to it."

"Is there someone you love? Some special woman?"

"No," he said. "Not now."

Margaret Way takes great pleasure in her work and works hard at her pleasure. She enjoys tearing off to the beach with her family on weekends, loves haunting galleries and auctions, and is completely given over to French champagne "for every possible joyous occasion." Her home, perched high on a hill overlooking Brisbane, Australia, is her haven. She started writing when her son was a baby, and now she finds there is no better way to spend her time.

Books by Margaret Way

Don't miss any of our special offers. Write to us at the following address for information on our newest releases.

Harlequin Reader Service
901 Fuhrmann Blvd., P.O. Box 1397, Buffalo, NY 14240
Canadian address: P.O. Box 603,
Fort Erie, Ont. L2A 5X3

Morning Glory
Margaret Way

Harlequin Books

TORONTO • NEW YORK • LONDON
AMSTERDAM • PARIS • SYDNEY • HAMBURG
STOCKHOLM • ATHENS • TOKYO • MILAN

Original hardcover edition published in 1988
by Mills & Boon Limited

ISBN 0-373-02939-X

Harlequin Romance first edition October 1988

CHAPTER ONE

THE SUN woke her; the sun, the birds and the heady incenselike smell of flowers. Kit flung a smooth golden arm across her eyes as sunlight pierced the Persian-pink shutters and made rainbows across her bed. Dawn in the tropics was glorious, a miraculous illumination that transformed the pearly dimness of her room between darkness and dawn into a golden pavilion. Kit turned languorously and looked around her, entranced by the rare light. She had created her own special environment, but it took the sun to wrap it in shimmering veils. Now the blush pink, mauve and gold were shot through with apricot, as fingers of sunlight rayed through the sheer curtains. Instants of glory! She responded with all the passionate sense of beauty inherent in an artistic and sensuous nature.

It was shortly after five— time to luxuriate and enjoy the birdsong and fragrance, the sheer joy of being young and at one with the morning. She curled her bare toes against the smooth sheet that covered her, stretching and stretching until she reminded herself of the slowly unfolding bromeliad, 'Heart of Flame', that grew in great masses in the open garden.

Even in the cool of dawn, the air was heavy with sweet spicy scent: ginger blossom, King Jasmine, gardenia, the creamy frangipani and the intoxicating oleanders. The combined bouquet was so powerful, so stimulating, it was an aphrodisiac: clean, natural, yet unbelievably sensuous.

It made her body ache in new, mysterious ways, filling her with yearnings she had never been conscious of before. Childhood, for the fortunate, was a carefree, happy period. Adolescence, ideally, was calm and stable, but lately she had been subjected to many an upheaval.

5

She had never anticipated the swift development of her sexuality. It was almost as though she had a new body, one that ached for the touch of a lover's hand. The bud had turned into the flower and her girlish innocence was being submerged by increasing pressures. A lot of her thoughts and dreams were of romantic encounters. She arched her back spontaneously and a rush of blood made a radiance of her flawless skin.

At nineteen, she was aroused, ready for love. Nothing senseless, but bold, passionate, real, an experience that would catch her up fiercely, heart, body, mind. Without love, one was nothing. *Nothing*. Kit breathed a name. Was it even a real name? Her arms lifted from her side, as though a lean male figure loomed above to embrace her. She was ready, ready... burning, shaking...

The excruciating part was, there was no one there.

Kit gave a gurgle like a crystal bell in her throat. So much for her silken dreams! She sprang out of bed in readiness to confront her day. It wasn't the first time lately she had begun to fantasise about the man. She had certain requirements; in fact, he was clearly defined in her mind. He would be full of strength and character; a leader, not a follower. He did not have to be handsome, but he had to be full of humour and honest. He would love her in exactly the way she wanted, and her passion for him would never be assuaged. He would be a man on the move. A doer herself, she knew a layabout would be unworthy of her attention. She saw him as dark, preferably with fine dark eyes—a latter-day Sean Connery, perhaps. Kit was physically attracted to dark, powerful men. The fair-haired men of her experience tended to be too cool or too boyish. He would have to be tall, preferably over six feet. She couldn't risk a little guy, no matter how macho. Above average height herself, she would hate never to be able to wear high heels. No one could put her down about her legs, though she had been raised to believe her looks lacked all class and subtlety. Someone had to take responsibility for that, but it wasn't her darling Paddy or her mother. Obviously she was a throwback. Or maybe not. A changeling?

A breeze banged the shutter against the wall, and Kit stepped out on to the veranda to fix it. She always took care of things immediately they happened. 'Blatant' in appearance she might be, but she was the most domesticated of young women. She loved her home, the garden, fixing things, sewing, cooking. She was very competent, really. A pity Clare, her mother, wasn't the encouraging sort.

Down in the glorious controlled wilderness of the terraced gardens, hundreds of brilliant little lorikeets were whistling and shrieking as they plundered the nectar from millions of flowery throats. She lived in paradise, which made her even more conscious of her metamorphosis from innocent child to palpitating, quivering woman. Her sensibilities almost overnight had been raised to fever pitch. Even in her mundane moments, there was an undertone of excitement in her, as though she was moving inexorably towards immense new adventures.

Her exuberance, her zest for life, her mother thought to be dangerous. Clare was always hinting that Kit would wind up in some mess. Perhaps she would, but she knew she could depend on herself to get out of it. Some people went through life fingering out the costs, others took life by the throat. She couldn't go forever doing precisely what her mother expected of her. When she was younger she had ached with bewilderment and confusion, but these days she had to accept things as they were. She could never win her mother's love, or at least the level of love and approval that was lavished on Melanie. Then again, Melly was as near perfect as any sister could wish. She was beautiful, pure, truthful. She was extraordinarily amiable and never given to confrontations. She had never been heard to utter a rude word. Her mind wasn't terribly well developed—but then, what man rated intelligence above beauty? Perhaps Melly paid a little bit too much attention to her mirror. But given her blonde beauty, why not? She *was* lazy—yes, definitely lazy, like some exquisitely indolent chinchilla Persian. Melly knew exactly how to take care of herself. Anyway, what did it all matter? Kit loved them all.

Patrick, her father, was her favourite, for all her mother called him a drop-out. At such times, Patrick only grinned engagingly and commented that he hadn't chosen a bad little place to drop out. Plenty of other people opted out of the rat-race, he told them. He wasn't eager to die of an early heart attack.

It was Patrick who had built their rain-forest home—that alone showed the great natural ability of the man. It was a marvellously well oriented and picturesque place; almost a child's conception of how a house should look, with a wonderful sloping roof and wide deep verandas. The walls were of timber, there were lots of huge picture windows, and the whole had a happy aura of being at peace with the environment. Kit boasted about her father endlessly. He was a gifted man, yet somehow, somewhere, he had lost all worldly ambition. Now that she had grown up, Kit began to question many of the things Patrick appeared to say in jest. Something about Patrick tore at her. She had the dismal feeling he was a man perpetually under constraint. Something in life had disrupted his plans. Much as he denied it, Kit was a girl of considerable intuition, and she knew Patrick so well.

A vagrant breeze caught the curtain, almost toppling a delicate porcelain flamingo. Kit, with her quick reflexes, fielded it deftly and placed it out of harm's way. Her room was filled with a fine array of art objects. In fact, it was a very pleasing and comfortable room altogether. She had made the lovely floral-patterned chintz bedspread and the filmy curtains, even the plump lavishly trimmed cushions. She wanted everything about her to be right, or as right as she could make it. Anyone could sit around doing nothing. Kit never overlooked an opportunity to use her creative abilities or her initiative. It was she, as self-appointed family business manager, who had hit on the idea of a gallery for Patrick; somewhere harmonious where people could see his pottery and paintings. Because these days Patrick's main consideration wasn't work, she had persuaded other local artists—potters, wood-carvers, painters, silversmiths and tapestry-makers—to exhibit at the gallery for a small commission. The whole venture was becoming increasingly successful, for Kit, though she didn't give herself much credit, had tremendous style and a positive genius for positioning art works for maximum effect. She even had plans in hand to build a rotunda-style coffee shop in the magnificent grounds, if only she could talk Patrick round. The increasing number of tourists had to be catered for, but Patrick seemed strangely loath to capitalise on the gallery's spreading reputation.

'We could lose all anonymity,' he had told her, and Kit had been startled by the degree of feeling in his voice, a real anxiety. What had Patrick to be anxious about? He'd either become reclusive or he really did have something to hide. It was all very disquieting. The more Kit thought about it, the more she reached the unwelcome conclusion that there just could be genuine cause for concern. Patrick had turned completely from the life of successful surveyor to develop his skills in the art world. Admittedly, he had chosen an artists' colony to do it in, but as far away from civilisation as he could get. Kit hadn't fully realised this until about her fourteenth birthday, when what had seemed the most marvellous life-style suddenly struck her as an eternal holiday. The best life wasn't the easiest life. Patrick couldn't even keep himself fully occupied. She was no nearer an answer at nearing twenty than she had been at fourteen, no nearer to the cause of Clare's increasing flashes of bitterness. Underneath the tropical dream was a melodrama—a secret too difficult to tell?

Kit rested her cheek against the vine-wreathed timber post. It was covered with the sweet-smelling pink flowers she adored. She had favourite moments of the day, and this was one of them. Nature never failed to impart a blessed peace of its own. Patrick wasn't at peace—not quite. Patrick assured her that their background couldn't have been more ordinary, only he wasn't an ordinary man. He was a man who pretended to be ordinary, as though it were folly to be anything else. Once, Kit had gripped his arm and tried to force something out of him,

but he had only bellowed with laughter, his wonderful
sea-blue eyes sparkling, yet curiously non-reflective.

'You're like me, m'darling. You have a craving for
drama.'

Drama? So why, then, had Patrick chosen a life of
obscurity? For one instant, heart pounding, Kit thought
it had something to do with herself. She felt it intensely,
but it was patently absurd. She loved Patrick. She loved
him very deeply, and their little confrontations always
ended in the same way. He always managed to turn her
many questions aside. It was impossible to draw Clare
into these discussions. Clare only looked at them with
cool grey eyes. In effect, she withdrew from any discussion of the past. There wasn't a moment when she
weakened, so nothing was ever resolved to Kit's peace
of mind.

Kit stared down at the water. Through the feathery
line of casuarinas, the beach glinted white, and beyond
that were the wonderful opal colours of the cove. The
sky was already a perfect cloudless turquoise and the
crystal-clear water ranged through a wide spectrum of
jewel colours: jade in the shallows, a long stretch of glittering aqua, heart-of-emerald, and beyond the white-
capped secret reef, deepest, glowing sapphire.

She hurried back into her room and scooped up one
of her minuscule bikinis in cobalt blue and hot pink. She
had a whole wardrobe of them, for she had made them
all herself. She found herself looking into the mirror at
her naked body. She was an all-over tawny gold, except
for the briefest V-shaped patch at the juncture of her
thighs. Sunbathing topless on their own secluded beach
was one thing, but she had never risked total nudity.
Normally, she dressed with her back to the mirror, but
now something made her take a good long look at herself.
She was long-limbed, fine-boned, small-breasted. Her
waist was even tiny. Her hips were taut and slender, and
her legs went on for ever. It wasn't Melanie's figure, she
thought, petite, rounded, but some people, most people,
would probably consider it a whole lot better. Melly had

to give thought to what she ate, Kit tended to lose weight rather than gain it. Her figure would definitely hold up.

Her face. She stared at herself so hard she began to squint. It was odd really that her looks should turn her mother so much against her. 'To me, you're perfect!' Patrick would often say, but she wasn't at all what Clare had wanted or expected. 'You really want to play down that flamboyant look, Kit,' Clare frequently exhorted her. 'Your colouring is quite enough.'

Her colouring *was* theatrical, she had to admit it. She had never seen her exact shade of hair before, a singularly rich russet. With hair that colour she might have expected either Patrick's or Clare's fine, very fair skin, but her skin was almost olive and it took a beautiful, even tan. Odder yet, her brows and lashes were an emphatic black and her eyes, though blue like Patrick's, darkened into violet. When she was a little girl, Patrick had always taken her up on his shoulder, calling her his Morning Glory. She truly only felt acceptance from her father. Perhaps she was ungrateful to expect more?

Two minutes later, with her white-fringed beach towel draped around her slender hips and a hibiscus flower behind her ear, Kit made her way along the grassy path flanked by a myriad varieties of palms and luxuriant stands of banana trees, through the brilliant beds of flowers to the beach. In her favoured secluded spot between two splendid pyramid-shaped dunes, she dropped her towel and broke into a spiralling run of joy. For the young, each second had to be lived, and Kit was only just beginning to grasp that she had a vibrant lust for life.

By the time she hit the water, her eyes were dazzled by the undulating sea of sequins. She only surfaced for air before diving deep again. Water was no barrier; she was almost as much at home in the sea as Oskar, her pet dolphin. Oskar had been coming right into the cove ever since the afternoon of her seventh birthday, when he had suddenly appeared like some magical messenger. Kit could still remember that day of brilliant happiness, looking out over the water while Oskar had swum right

up to her. The five-year-old dimpled Melly had screamed
and fallen in fright to the sand. Patrick, astounded, had
leapt to her, his apprehension miraculously melting as
it became apparent that this was no porpoise but the
legendary dolphin, sacred to the god Apollo. Moreover,
this dolphin was seemingly trying to communicate with
his child. That had been the beginning of their amazing
friendship. Kit could not have wished for more devotion
from a sea creature. In many ways, Oskar responded
like a dog, obeying calls and whistles, fetching and
throwing rubber balls and leaping around her in an ecstasy of joy. Kit even boasted that she had taught him
to talk. There was no question, 'good boy' came out as
clear as a bell.

There was no sign of Oskar this morning. She rarely
saw him then; late afternoon was their time for sporting.
Kit turned on her back and floated. Her reverence for
beauty, for nature, was intense. This was one of the last
wilderness areas of the world: tropical North
Queensland, a paradise of luxuriant green rain-forest,
purple mountains with peaks for ever shrouded in mist,
crater lakes, gorges and waterfalls and endless miles of
white sandy beaches and glorious turquoise seas.

No wonder her heart was bursting with an urgent
hunger! This was a world that pulsed with golden opu-
lence. The kiss of the sun and sea was incredibly sweet,
but this new awareness craved the kiss of a man who
loved her. Passion was a wonderful thing.

On the beach she went into a series of balletic exer-
cises, luxuriating in the suppleness of her young body.
She was something of a fitness freak, unlike Melly who,
though enchantingly pretty, was ever so slightly plump.
Melly still called their mother 'Mummy', though Clare
had long since let it be known that she preferred Kit to
call her by her Christian name. Kit thought of herself
as the odd woman out. It made her feel sad. Surely
'Mother' was the most beautiful name in the world?

A light plane went by overhead, probably making for
one of the Great Barrier Reef islands. The Reef, the most
remarkable coral reef system in the world and a fabu-

lous playground for tourists, stretched offshore some two thousand kilometres along the Queensland coast. As Kit spread out her towel, she looked directly out on several coral cays, almost perfect emerald rings, encircled by dazzling white and floating in that glorious sapphire sea. It was all so beautiful, it hurt.

In the shelter of the dunes she discarded her tiny bra and exposed her almost naked body to the sun. Swimming and sunbathing surely had to be among the more pure earthly delights. She dug her toes into the sand, glorious moment, feeling the exhilaration of superb physical fitness. She smiled when she thought of Melly's aversion to exercise. 'I don't know how you can cook yourself, either,' Melly always added. Kit *didn't* cook herself; she allowed the sun to dry her off before she began collecting shells for the Sea Cave—another one of her ideas, and mainly to give Melanie something to do. Their mother wouldn't allow Melly to help her in the store, but she had no objection to Melanie presiding dreamily over the delightful nook Kit had incorporated into the gallery. Kit even permitted the continuing myth that it was Melanie who had dreamed it all up and Melanie's pretty fingers that devised the lovely shell bouquets and engaging little fun objects the tourists, even the locals, swooped on in droves.

In many ways, I've taken over the traditional male role, Kit thought, which was probably why her relationship with Clare was becoming increasingly difficult. Clare didn't care for Kit's 'exuberance' or what she called Kit's 'unfeminine drive and aggressiveness'. Such criticisms, though they were generally accepted with humour, really hurt Kit deeply. Didn't Clare realise the benefits Kit's unfeminine drive had bought them? It seemed not. Nowadays, they were forever at odds, not in any fierce and vocal fashion, but something quiet and deep. Longing to be loved by her mother, Kit thought it had to be *her* fault. No one could fail to love Melly, but she wasn't faultless. They would all starve if it were left to Melly to provide. It was a strange household if indolence met with approval and industry was labelled aggression. Perhaps she *was* too positive. Melly was all softness and serenity. Even Patrick found it restful.

'My flame and my flower', Patrick called them, yet it was only in the last year that he had painted a portrait of them together. It was so startlingly good, so totally unlike the extraordinary and colourful abstracts that took up all his studio space, Kit was concerned that he wasn't realising his potential. Why had he never attempted a portrait before or since?

When she had asked, Clare's cool grey eyes had openly challenged them. 'Ask your father to show you his masterpiece some time,' she challenged.

'I would, my darling, only I've long since destroyed it.'

Kit just knew her father had been lying, though nothing had been allowed to ripple the calm surface of his eyes. Portraits became a dangerous topic and, ever sensitive to her mother's withdrawals, Kit had wisely dropped the subject. Had the portrait been of Clare? Had it not pleased her? Clare was a woman of considerable reserve, but her feelings went very deep. She loved Patrick even now with passion, for all they were as different as the proverbial chalk and cheese. They had all been so much closer in the old days, before Kit's cycle of adolescence began. Now, terribly, Kit sometimes thought her mother couldn't stand her, or, if that were too much, the simple sight of her. Her looks did not please. It was Melanie who closely resembled their mother. As far as Kit could see, she didn't resemble anyone at all, not even her beloved Patrick. Heaven help her, she was only *herself*!

She didn't hear the drag of footsteps in the sand until they were almost upon her. She tilted her head back, expecting to see only Melly delicately devouring a mango. Instead, her whole body jumped in a state of sweeping shock.

A man was standing in utter stillness, staring down at her. Her first impression was that he was fantastically tall, lean to the point of attenuation, yet she never doubted he was physically strong. His clothes, though good quality, were a far cry from his remarkable aura. They were everyday-casual: dark stretched jeans and a collarless linen shirt carelessly buttoned. Something gold glittered from the wall of his chest, a medallion of some kind that looked oddly battered. His thick hair was almost long, dark blond streaked with gold and brushed back from a proud, hard face of clean-cut arrogant features. The cheekbones were sharp, with shadowed hollows. He had a fine straight nose and a chiselled mouth. There was a severity to him that almost caught Kit's breath. But the most compelling thing about him was his eyes: impenetrable, yet looking through and beyond her. Moreover, they were a rare, flawless topaz, like some exotic unblinking cougar. His magnetism was so powerful, Kit's considerable native courage almost deserted her. She gave an involuntary gasp, and continued to lie there like a creature bereft of will.

She felt not only stripped of her clothing, all artifice, but her skin. Years later, she would remember the intensity of those moments. He might have been a statue, so arrested was his pose, yet Kit felt a sudden rush of adrenalin course through her blood. Her shuddering breath shook her torso and lifted her delicate breasts.

'Forgive me—I startled you.'

His voice, at least, was normal. Instead of a low purr, it was cool, cultivated, very, very English. Kit whipped up, shaking out her towel and draping it across her embarrassing nakedness. 'This *is* a private beach,' she pointed out crisply, thinking she didn't know how she would ever forget this.

The topaz eyes narrowed. 'And where in the laws of the land does it say that?'

The slight grittiness made the inflammable Kit catch fire. 'The beach in front of our house we regard as our own,' she retorted.

'So the law is a matter of your interpretation?' His mouth curved ironically, withering her.

'Something of that sort.'

'Then you've lived too long on a frontier.'

'And I believe you're a stranger.' She bent and swept up the vivid scrap of her bra, intending to surge past him, but her body needed more time to break the crackling confusion.

'Would you please let me past?' she said coldly.

'Certainly.' He took a long, elegant step sideways and, in an ecstasy of anger, Kit staggered.

'Stop that! Don't be frightened.' The lean body rippled, and his hand clenched around her arm.

'I'm *not* frightened,' she gritted, staring as though mesmerised at his long, lean, brown fingers on the fine skin of her arm. 'Do you *mind*?'

He said nothing, but released her, his extraordinary eyes now totally absorbed in her face.

'What's your name?'

'What *is* this?' Her cheeks flamed and her violet eyes blazed. She was appalled at the storm he had let loose in her.

'I expect you have a name?'

'And why ever would I give you that information? We're strangers, and strangers we'll remain.'

'If it's a secret, I'll find out.'

Kit was totally disconcerted. Despite her embarrassing déshabillée, she could have sworn her femininity held no interest for him. 'I'd like to go,' she said stonily.

'I'm not stopping you.' He shrugged slightly, the most striking, the most elegant, the most *hateful* man she had ever seen.

'Have a nice day,' she added caustically.

'I plan to. Perhaps you could tell me which *is* the Beach Trail.'

'The other side of the cove.' Now she stood above him, free of that tallness, that leanness.

'One might hope the natives are more friendly.'

That very English upper class drawl really got to her.

'I'm sure you'd scare anybody,' she snapped.

'But you're not scared, have you forgotten?'

She heard the dispassionate mockery of his tone, then the focus changed. Kit was a very observant young woman and she detected strain, even exhaustion, behind the unassailable self-possession.

'I do hope I haven't ruined your morning,' she said more quietly, on the outside all flaunting beauty, inside highly sensitive. A gauzy winged insect lodged in her curling mane and she lifted a hand to it, the swift graceful action firming her exquisite young breasts.

His topaz eyes slid from her radiant head to her long gilded legs. 'You haven't disturbed me in any way.'

'Same here!' she assured him tartly. 'If you're taking a stroll tomorrow, you might go the other way.'

'And a word of advice to you, young lady,' he called after her in a clipped, inflammatory tone. 'The world, even *this* world, is not what you think. I wouldn't continue to sunbathe near-naked in isolated spots.'

Kit refused to turn her head. *Isolated spots!* She was almost in front of her own home. Well, it *was* isolated. Why else would she sunbathe there? It's all right, she told herself. All right. Keep calm. Fleet-footed as a gazelle, she had difficulty climbing the terraced slopes. Maybe she needed that kind of encounter to tell her she couldn't handle every situation as she had foolishly thought. Nothing in life had prepared her for that man's magnetism; it was as powerful as a weapon. She even felt as though she had crashed into some dangerous force field. It wasn't as though in the last few years she hadn't met plenty of people, crowds of them in the tourist season. All ages, all walks of life, even the super-rich and internationally famous. She just didn't *believe* in that man!

Melanie caught sight of her as she surged through the door.

'Oh, my gosh, Kit, you know you're not supposed to come into the house without your top on. Mummy doesn't like it.'

Melly was descending the stairs, the modern version of Juliet: flaxen hair falling straight to her shoulders, big grey eyes luminous, a silky robe clinging lovingly to her nubile body.

'Hi! You look great!' Kit called with a look of amused admiration. 'Don't worry, in another second I'll be in my room. Nudity is indeed a secret thing.'

'At least I'd grab a blouse,' said Melanie.

'Go on! You're proud of your cute little bosoms. Not so little, actually,' added Kit.

'You're just jealous,' Melly smirked. 'Say, is anything wrong?'

Was it that apparent? 'Of course not,' Kit answered. 'I tripped coming up the hill.'

'You will take it so fast,' Melly clicked with a certain satisfaction. 'Couldn't you find any shells this morning?'

'Didn't look.'

'Well, you should,' Melly pointed out earnestly. 'I sell so many every day.'

'What do you say?' Kit challenged her, as they passed on the stairs. 'Try collecting some yourself. It's getting so I have no free time.'

'You will take so much on yourself,' Melly answered sweetly, moving away.

Their mother, wearing a green kimono, stood on the first landing, listening.

'Is there any reason why you're using that tone of voice, Kit?' she demanded, sounding severe.

Both girls turned to look at her, upset by her mood.

'What tone of voice, Mum?' Kit, threw up her hands, hardly suited to passivity.

'*Clare,*' her mother corrected, cool grey eyes flinty. 'And you know very well what I mean. You don't imagine Melanie doesn't have things to do?'

'No big deal, Mummy,' Melly begged soothingly. 'There's no reason why I don't collect the shells except that Kit's the expert. You know, I've never forgotten that awful sting I got from one of the conches.'

'You don't have to risk your pretty fingers. I'll get them,' said Kit with unthinking irony.

'I believe I've asked you, Kit, not to walk around half naked. Sunbathe topless if you must, but don't come into the house looking like that,' Clare continued inexorably.

'I'm sorry, Clare. I really forgot.'

'The story of your life, Kit,' Clare sighed. 'You don't *want* to do what I tell you.'

Kit fled.

'Would you like a pineapple juice?' Melly asked her when she returned to snatch her breakfast.

'Lovely, thank you.'

'I really don't think you have to wait on your sister,' Clare said sharply.

'Why are you always angry, Clare?' Kit beseeched. She put down the glass Melly had passed her and held out her hand.

'My dear Kit,' Clare protested, never relinquishing a mixing bowl, 'I don't think I ever raise my voice.'

'But you're angry underneath. I know you love me, but I can't *feel* your love.'

'How ridiculous, Kit!' Clare replied irritably.

'I know what she means, Mummy.' Melly sat down on a chair, looking flushed and grave. 'You don't have to yell to let us know you're mad. You *are* different— even I can see that. Am I going to have to stop calling you Mummy now I'm nearly eighteen? I don't want to have to call you Clare like Kit. Kit won't admit it, but it really kills her.'

Clare's fine white brow darkened and she looked bleak. 'It seemed like a good idea now Kit's grown up to call me Clare,' she pointed out almost cuttingly. '*You're* my little girl, my baby.'

'And you treat us so differently,' Kit protested quietly.

'Because you are so different,' Clare replied starkly. 'Don't act as if I'm inflicting some terrible hurt on you, Kit. I've been a good mother to you.'

'Yes, of course you have,' Kit whispered, pale under her golden tan. 'Well, I'd better go. There's never a morning someone isn't waiting for me at the store.'

'Please, Kit, can't you have a bit more breakfast?' Melly looked at her sister anxiously. 'It's important, a good breakfast.'

'You should know, kitten.' Kit smiled gratefully. 'It's all right, Melly, don't worry, I'll have a carton of milk for lunch.'

'Those colours really don't go together,' Clare called after her.

'Gosh, Mummy, is this something you can't control?' cried Melly, with a wobble in her voice. 'Kit looks terrific—she always does.'

'I simply said those two colours don't really match.' With amazement, Kit saw there were tears in Clare's cool grey eyes. Tears because Melly was maturing and assuming a stronger stand in relation to her sister.

'Maybe they don't,' Kit supplied soothingly, 'but nobody minds at the store. By the way, Melly, some of us are going to the hideaway tonight, want to come?'

Melly's grey eyes lit up. 'You bet! Maybe Rick Knowles will fall in love with me. He's never seen me at my best.'

'You never think to consult me first, do you, Kit?' Clare intervened wrathfully, setting the bowl of whipped eggs down so abruptly, that the bowl gave an ominous dull crack.

'You must be joking, Mummy,' Melly pleaded, making a sound between a laugh and a sob. 'I'll be eighteen soon. You don't expect me to stay at home every night.'

Clare gave a bark of scornful laughter. 'It's just unbelievable! Suddenly *Kit* is running your life!'

'Please, Clare, it's not like that at all,' said Kit earnestly.

'You be quiet, Kit. All right?'

Kit was so incensed and upset she lost her temper. 'It's impossible to talk to you, Mum!' she snapped angrily.

'If you'd like to leave, feel free.'

'Oh, Mummy!' Melly wailed.

'You should be proud, Kit,' said Clare.

'You expect me to apologise? I'm pleased to. I do it all the time, except that I don't know what I'm doing wrong.'

'So innocent!' sneered her mother.

'Innocent, my foot! If you'd just tell me.'

'No, thanks.'

'*Oh!*' Kit's vital voice took on a colourless tone. 'I try so hard, you can't imagine.'

'That's touching, Kit, but you should give more thought to what you say and do. No one could call you sensitive. *I* am Melanie's mother. Please refer to me.'

'You mean my own *sister* can't ask me anywhere?' Melly asked, aghast. 'You'd think she was suggesting a life of crime!'

A clear melodious snatch of whistling, something from *Carmen*, floated through the window, and the jangle of women's voices ceased immediately.

Patrick Lacey, looking the popular conception of an artist, walked into the kitchen, greeting them all warmly.

'A brilliant day, my beauties!' he exclaimed with satisfaction. 'I want an easel set up on the lawn. I say, Kit,' he exclaimed admiringly, 'I envy your eye for colour. It's impeccable.' He grabbed his younger daughter lightheartedly, and kissed her cheek resoundingly. 'Is my breakfast ready, angel?'

'Almost, Daddy.' Melly leant against him adoringly. 'Kit says she'll take me out with her tonight. Can I go?'

'*May* I go, and after I've given proper thought to the matter,' he teased her. 'Can't talk you into staying home today, Kit?'

'Eden Cove would be without a general store,' Kit pointed out.

'It's sad that you've tied yourself up there,' Patrick sighed solemnly, lowering himself into a chair.

'It was a stroke of good fortune at the time.' Kit glanced briefly at her watch. 'I need to make some money, remember?' *We* needed the extra money, she thought, but kindly refrained from adding.

'It's degrading,' Clare added, as she always did on these occasions. 'You have artistic ability. Why don't you stay home with your father and learn his craft?'

'She's learned most of it already,' Patrick said cheerfully, and stroked his full, curling beard. 'No, really, Kit has made things change completely. Who would have ever thought the gallery would be such a success? Of course,' he assumed an arch air, 'who wouldn't drop in to catch sight of *this* vision?'

'Tell me more, Daddy,' Melly coaxed him, and grabbed his arm. Kit stood silently for a moment, watching them.

'If you've got a little time this afternoon, I'd like you to listen to a few more of my ideas,' she exhorted him.

'Please, darling, nothing that involves work,' Patrick threw up his large arms.

'Work doesn't do anyone any harm,' Kit answered cheerfully. 'Speaking of which, I must leave on the spot.'

CHAPTER TWO

KIT CYCLED down to the small general store, the only one Eden Cove boasted, and when she arrived two customers were waiting for her: Signora Campigli, a privileged dowager in her late fifties, and the accident-prone six-year-old Jimmy Cox. Each of them was studying the other with some suspicion and a modicum of aggression.

'A fine time to run out of coffee, Christiana,' the Signora called to her in her big, beautiful, incongruously sexy voice. Patrick loved it.

'*I* was here first,' Jimmy reminded her, personage or not.

'You want I should wait for a child?'

'Please—both of you, come in.' Soothingly, Kit smiled and opened up. 'What *did* you want, Jimmy?'

'Some cigarettes for Mum.'

The Signora wheezed her disgust.

'Sure.' Kit reached for a packet. It always affected her that Jimmy was sent on the same errand, but what could she do, refuse to sell them to him? Maybe she would next time. Jimmy was an uncommonly adventurous child; he could start lighting up.

'Mum says can she book them up?' he grinned.

At least for a little while longer, Kit thought. 'All right, Jimmy. How did you come to injure your leg?'

While Jimmy launched into a fantastic tall story, the Signora rolled her eyes.

'The little rascal!' she huffed, after Jimmy had been sent off with a stick of liquorice. 'You should not encourage him.'

'Try living with his family,' grimaced Kit.

'*Si*, one has to be grateful.' The Signora touched a hand to her monumental bosom. 'The mother, you think—a little light retardation?'

23

Kit was treated to a story about a cousin whose brains had been affected by the inhalation of nicotine fumes. 'By the way, Christiana, you know we have a stranger in town. A ve-e-ry important man.'

'Really?' Kit switched off the coffee grinder and looked back with interest. There was nothing that went on that the Signora didn't know about. 'Who?'

Signora Campigli heaved herself complacently into the nearest chair. 'You must know him, if only by reputation. A little more of that lovely cheese,' she leaned forward, smacking her lips in appreciation. 'The way you have improved this place, Christiana, has been like magic. I dislike to see you, so beautiful, so clever, hidden away from the world. You should be continuing your education, so you can mix in the highest circles.'

'I fantasise about it, Signora,' Kit smiled.

'I worry about you,' the Signora frowned. 'Your family do not appreciate what they have! You are not one of those girls who amount to nothing. You have a sense of adventure, excitement, such marvellous energy. Your paintings, you know, are so much better than dear Patrick's. No, Christiana, do not protest. Where would your family be without you?'

'Probably better off in a sense. I can't change my metabolism.'

'And such character!' Signora Campigli ignored this.

'I thought you were going to tell me the name of our mystery visitor?'

'Absolutely!' The Signora's liquid black eyes flashed. 'Thorne Stratton,' she announced with a snort of triumph.

'I recognise it. Just barely.' Kit finished wrapping up the cheese.

'Why, Christiana, think for a moment longer.'

'A film star?'

The Signora pulled heavily on her rings. 'Very much better than that. This man is a lion!'

'A *lion*?' Something clicked strongly inside Kit's head.

'Not some actor playing a part. No Rambo! This man has been in the very front line. He has paid dearly for his bravery.'

'How very peculiar indeed,' said Kit drily.

'Well?'

'Well, what?'

'Why are you looking so stricken, so shocked?'

Kit blushed in recollection. 'I think I've met the great man,' she explained.

'Christiana!' The Signora was so startled, she picked up a fresh bun and thrust it into her mouth. 'He has called here?'

'I'd be greatly relieved if he had. No, I met him on the beach.' Kit sighed heavily. 'This very morning.'

'You were sunbathing?' Signora Campigli asked, giving Kit a meaningful stare.

'By rights, he ought not to have stumbled on me.'

The Signora brushed a few crumbs from her cheeks. 'He must have seen you as a goddess,' she observed.

Kit gave a sharp sniff of derision. 'Sorry—I made no impression at all. Except for a second, when he actually demanded my name.'

'Certainly,' the Signora nodded vigorously.

'I didn't give it.'

'It's of no importance. He will surely come to the store.'

'If he does,' Kit said briskly, 'I'll be wearing a mask.'

Much as she tried, Kit couldn't control a nervous start every time a vehicle pulled up outside the store. It didn't do much for her self-esteem, but it was better than closing shop. There was even the chance that he wouldn't know her in her clothes, only he had been amazingly interested in her face. Perhaps he wouldn't come to the store at all. But he had to eat. She sighed, almost worn out with her speculations, tore a carton in two, tossed the pieces in the air, caught them neatly and deposited them in the bin. She vowed never to sunbathe topless again. Nowhere in the world was safe. Even her own secluded beach had turned into a lively thoroughfare!

Her regulars came in in a nice steady stream, bought a few things, caught up on the local gossip and left.

'Kit,' she said to herself, 'stay cool. He won't come.'

By mid-afternoon she had almost finished carrying the latest deliveries to the rear of the store when, as chance would have it, a cobalt-blue Jaguar purred to a stop right outside the door. It was the kind of vision Kit had been dreading, now she missed it as she put a hand to her aching back. Patrick let her do it. They all let her do it. Still, she would act tough. That was how they measured her muscle.

'Good afternoon.'

The voice had already eaten into her mind. Kit snapped to attention, staring at the man who had simply materialised.

'I told you we'd meet again.'

'Really? I was praying we wouldn't meet for years to come.' Her haste to move was a mistake, because she almost knocked over a cardboard display figure and had to straighten it up.

'You're angry,' he smiled—a wonderful smile. 'I'm sorry if our...encounter caused you embarrassment.'

There were deep little creases like brackets at the sides of his chiselled mouth, so that when he smiled like that the severe power was transformed into something devastatingly sexy. On anyone else, it would have turned Kit into a rag doll, only she was firing like a finely tuned motor.

'You're not sorry at all,' she said crisply. 'You're the least sorry man I've ever seen!'

'Please,' he shrugged and held up an elegant, long-fingered hand. 'It's too hot to catch fire.'

'Fire? *Who?*' She opened her eyes and looked around. 'You.'

Kit gave a small laugh and refilled her coffee-cup. 'I believe you're fooled by the colour of my hair. I don't fully understand what it does to me, either. Now, you're here, so I presume you want something?'

'Indeed I do.' The creases around his mouth deepened. 'You might go and fetch the owner.'

'I guess that's deliberate.' Kit's rosy head came up.

'What is?' he drawled.

'You know darn well I'm in charge.'

'Now, how would I know that, little Miss...?'

'Lacey. Kit Lacey.' She leaned her wrists on the counter almost belligerently. 'The owners are overseas.'

'I see,' he murmured meaningfully, transferring his unnerving gaze around the bright, impeccably clean and tidy store. 'Perhaps I'll have to wait until they come back.'

'Then you'll get even thinner,' she pointed out. 'They'll be away for another three months.'

'And you're in charge?' He gave her another one of those amused, piercing looks. 'First job out of school?'

'Yes.'

'At least that's honest.'

'I'm always honest,' she assured him. 'I'm sorry if it bothers you. I have a number of jobs, actually. I'm something of an entrepreneur.'

'Why not?' he agreed mildly. 'It's all the go these days; only you looked very vulnerable carrying those cartons. I couldn't help noticing that you winced as you straightened up.'

Kit felt a rush of embarrassment. 'I'm strong, don't you worry,' she shrugged his comment off. 'Now, I do have an enormous amount to get through. What do you need?'

There was a little silence while he gazed down at her. 'Well done,' he murmured quietly, and his arrogant face softened. 'If you tell me what else has to be shifted, I'll do it before I go.'

'I guess about a thousand boxes!' She waved a careless hand. 'I won't break, you know. *I'll* do it, and I'll take my time. Is that a list?'

'You haven't told me what the Kit stands for.'

'I think it's better we don't get on too friendly a basis,' she shrugged.

'My dear, it's quite unnecessary to be so cagey. Beautiful as you are, I assure you you haven't gone to my head. I have absolutely no designs on teenagers.'

'You could have fooled me,' said Kit briskly, shaken by that 'beautiful'. 'You're interested in me, and I can't really say why.'

'I can't, either,' he agreed deeply, 'and the Kit is for?'

'Something absolutely preposterous,' she told him sweetly. 'May I have that list?'

'Certainly. You have a family?'

'Is this an interview?' Kit frowned over the list of requirements.

'You ever talk about yourself?'

'Not to strangers. You must be expecting lots of guests.'

'I am,' he told her drily. 'This weekend. Do you think you can handle it?'

'How many is lots?' she asked coolly, raising her blue-violet eyes.

'Spunky little thing, aren't you?'

'I'm not little at all,' she pointed out.

'You *look* little,' he told her.

'That's because you're so threateningly tall.'

'The best I can do is six three.'

'You're so lean, your height is exaggerated. When I first caught sight of you I thought you were a goddamn giant!'

'You haven't started swearing yet?' he asked her, his amber eyes gleaming.

'I don't swear at all.'

'That "goddamn" unsettled me, young lady,' he remarked. 'What *does* the Kit stand for, Miss Lacey? I mean to know.'

'Would you believe, Christiana?'

He stepped forward so quickly, she almost jumped back against the shelves. 'I thought you really cared to know?' she protested.

'Just a minute,' he said bluntly. *'Christiana?'*

'Nobody except an Italian lady friend of mine calls me anything else but Kit,' she told him.

He looked and he looked at her. One would have thought he was in the business of making faces. 'Have you lived here all your life?' he asked at last.

'Let's put it this way,' said Kit. 'Nothing about me could possibly warrant such avid curiosity. I thought you were on holiday?'

He gave an elegant shrug. 'It's not a name one hears often.'

'It's not a name I often use. Is this something personal with you?' she challenged him. 'Were you madly in love with a Christiana at one time?'

'Don't be impertinent,' he warned her. 'I've never been *madly* in love with anyone.'

'You should get started before you stop.'

He raised his brows, staring down his straight nose at her. 'You could be right at that. It's a miracle I'm here.'

'Yes.' The compassionate Kit hung her head and bit her lip. 'If we could just skip the third degree. I'm a nobody, I assure you.'

'But you aren't,' he murmured pensively. 'I'm much struck by your looks. I remember them from somewhere.'

'But how?' Kit countered, half aggrieved and half reasonable. 'When you're not covering the danger spots, I understand you live in a very grand world.'

'Except, Christiana, the world is quite extraordinarily small.'

'All of which has nothing to do with the business on hand.' Kit tried hard to overcome her growing agitation. 'I'm sure no one else has been so struck by my appearance.'

'*I'm* sure you've made any number of men catch their breath.'

It was so totally unexpected! Kit threw a startled look into his eyes but, incredibly, he appeared totally serious.

'Why do you look like that?' he questioned.

'I wouldn't have expected to be called *beautiful*.'

The little creases beside his mouth deepened. 'You don't think you are?'

'Good lord, no!'

'My child, I've seen a great deal of the world; a great many beautiful women, of all races. You'll have to adjust your thinking.'

'Well, then,' she said amiably, 'put it in writing and
I'll take it home.'

'And home would be the Eden Cove art gallery?
You're the little genius behind it?'

Kit looked at him, startled. 'I'd like to say I am, but
it wouldn't be true. It's my father who exhibits his work,
along with local artists. And it's my sister who's the
beauty in the family.'

'My God, another one who looks like you?' he
drawled.

'No, she doesn't look like me,' Kit shrugged impatiently. 'She's blonde and quite lovely. She runs the
Sea Cave. We sell shells as I—*we* find them, or made
up in all sorts of ways: floral baskets, sprays, orna-
ments, that sort of thing.'

He nodded with faint mockery. 'The housekeeper was
telling me this morning.'

'You're staying at Senator Gower's place, aren't you?'
Kit suddenly put two and two together.

'So tell me, how did you know that? I've just arrived.'

'I guessed,' she said brightly. 'It's empty for most of
the year, except for a few weeks at Christmas or when
the senator makes it available for friends. How come
you didn't send the caretakers down? They shop here,
Mrs Russell and her husband.'

'I decided to see you again,' he told her coolly. 'Even
with your clothes, I'd recognise you anywhere. Now,
listen to me, are you able to get in those provisions?'

'Simple,' she lied. He was the sort of man to get that
reaction. Glenn would have to help her, yet again. 'I'll
have them delivered to the house on Friday afternoon.'

'Can you do that? I have a car.'

'And I've a van. You must be expecting to have a great
time.'

'It seems it's time,' he said mildly.

All of a sudden, Kit was ashamed of herself. Here was
a man who had covered stories all over the world; a man
who went right into the danger zones. She remembered
it was he who had foiled an assassination attempt on
some South-East Asian diplomat's life and had been

badly wounded in doing so. Wasn't he entitled to convalesce and escape the horror?

'I'm sorry,' she said quietly. Just being with him gave her a strange, dangerous feeling.

'Don't be. I'm standing here.'

'I suppose so.' She stared at him, absorbing his compelling aura. 'You were in the news a lot when that car bomb exploded. I thought this morning that there was a kind of severity to you. Now I see it's because you've lived in a terrible world. Are you well now?'

'I'm fine,' he said edgily.

'Good.' She spoke just as crisply. 'Should I keep this list, do you think? If you autograph it, I'm bound to. On second thoughts, I'll accept an autographed copy of your first novel.'

'I'd no idea I'd written one.' His winged eyebrows rose.

'You should.' She made a business of consulting his list. 'I notice you haven't asked for any paper?'

'I'm going to sit in the sun and never move from my chair.'

'Not you,' she said decisively. 'You're a man of action. Besides, how could a gifted writer not turn out a novel? You know the world. Tell us all you've seen.'

'You like organising people?' he asked drily.

'Since you mention it, yes. It's probably my most telling characteristic.'

'If it is, be proud of it. The world is full of people who do nothing at all.' There was a hollow ring in his voice. 'Actually, little one, you've sharpened an idea. Writing is a kind of therapy.'

'What's more, it will take your mind off *me*.'

'I wouldn't think of it,' he countered. 'Now I tell you what I'm going to do. Ben Russell was complaining that he had little to do, so I'll send him down to lend you a hand.'

'No, thank you,' Kit quickly rejected the offer. 'Didn't I mention that I'm strong?'

'You did, but I understand it has more to do with being fiercely independent.'

'Worse still, I'm proud.'

'So *I'll* help you,' he said with a touch of hard impatience.

'You'll kill yourself.'

He rounded on her so quickly, she felt giddy. 'Not unless you stop me.' He picked up the first of the remaining cartons and began to walk towards the rear of the shop.

'You don't have to do this, really.' She followed him up.

'How old are you?' he demanded, ignoring her.

That startled her. She drew back in some caution, unsettled by his manner. She lifted her hand, smudging dust from a cardboard box on her apricot-tinted cheek. 'Thirty-two.'

'Start again.' He passed her, going back and forth, and making quick work of a back-breaking chore.

'I'll be twenty soon.'

'You're a very bright, original girl to live in such an isolated spot. Why aren't you continuing your education?'

'What *is* education?' she parried. 'One sees a lot, even here. I read a great deal—all sorts of things. Art, history, economics. On the other hand, I can't start a revolution by breaking with my family. They need me—or I think they need me. Maybe bossy people think in extremes.'

'And you're bossy? Who laid *that* on you?' He moved closer to her, and she felt such a frightening thrill she nearly cried out.

'I suppose part of your training is getting people to confide in you?' she said shakily.

'There's a contrast between your manner, personality and those little hang-ups. Your self-image, for one thing. What *is* your conception of female beauty?' His amber eyes touched her face.

'You'll know when you see my sister.'

'And she's been constantly held up to you as an example?'

Kit turned away without answering, moving blindly towards the stack of cartons.

'Leave that,' he ordered shortly. 'Surely the previous owners could run to a wheeled loader? You simply slide it under the cartons and wheel them around.'

'Ben Morrison could hold a steady job lifting grand pianos,' she smiled.

'Well, *you* couldn't.'

'Would you like a cold drink?' she asked to appease him.

'No, thank you.'

'Anyway, if there's something really heavy, my father shifts it,' Kit assured him.

'I'm going to make you a present of one of those loaders.' He spoke without looking up, and Kit could see the rippling muscles of his body. She understood what it would be like for a man like him to have his superb body violated. No wonder there was strain behind the cool façade!

'This is ridiculous, you coming in and doing all the work!' She gave an exasperated sigh.

'I've explained to you that once you get the loader it won't have to happen again. Where else do you go after the Morrisons get back? Another shop lined up—hardware, fruit stall?'

'Am I supposed to deduce that shop assistants have no status?'

'Don't exaggerate. It just seemed to me, you're capable of a great deal more.'

'I can type,' she said sweetly, 'if you find yourself without a secretary.'

'However well you type, you couldn't type better than I.'

'If you didn't have to bother with the donkey work you could go a lot faster,' she countered.

'Miss Lacey, you make it sound very attractive, but I'm here to recuperate. If you wanted a little extra money, you could help out on Saturday nights. I haven't had time to assess Mrs Russell's various talents, but I have noticed she's a slow mover. I would say she could do with some help.'

'Possibly.' Kit blew a stray curl from her face. 'I don't know that I'm prepared to wait at your table.'

'You'd rather cook?'

'Mrs Russell is a marvellous cook!' she declared.

'I know that. She admires you as well. It was her idea, actually, that you join her. I believe you've done it before?'

'That was for friends,' Kit pointed out tartly.

'Why narrow the field? This is for money. Isn't that the whole point of being an entrepreneur?'

'I'm not completely sure about your motives,' she said slowly. 'You want something from me.'

'Of course. I want to know who you are.'

'I'm Kit Lacey,' she challenged him. She felt off balance, as from too much excitement.

'You're Christiana,' he corrected.

'Is it even a *real* name?'

'It's an unusual name. Like a princess.'

'Except I was born in the suburbs.'

'Not here?' He looked down without expression, the slanting sun catching the gilt streaks in his hair.

She sighed. 'Haven't we exhausted this subject?'

'On the contrary, Miss Lacey, I'm certain there are many things to discover about you.'

'You sound as if you're expecting to.' Close to, his inherent sexuality, so disregarded yet so potent, made her dizzy.

'I thought you wanted me to?'

All at once she couldn't cope. She saw his gleaming eyes, so intent on her face. 'This is crazy.' she said sharply. 'If Mrs Russell wants me to help her on Saturday, I'll do it. I'll expect twelve dollars an hour for my trouble. I imagine I'm expected to wear some kind of uniform. I have a black skirt and a white blouse. Beyond that, I have nothing to say.'

'Not even thank you?'

'Yes, thank you.' She gave in gracefully. 'It's impossible to have an easy conversation with you, but I do appreciate what you've done. It must be marvellous sometimes to be a man.'

He gave her another one of his cool, unnerving inspections. 'God forbid! Anyway, some women just demand to be swept off their feet. Not the clinging vines, as you might have thought, but the women that excite men the most—the bright, the brave, the resourceful.'

It was hours before Kit's breathing began to even out.

Kit locked up at five and took the unreliable van for a run out to the Cowley fruit farm. Glenn, her good friend from childhood, had been running it almost single-handed since his father had been killed in a terrible tree-felling accident on a neighbouring property. Bill Cowley had been a much liked, well respected man, and the whole district had been desolated, but none more than his widow, Sarah. Sarah Cowley's grief had been cemented by an abiding anger that caused their once good friends and neighbours, the McCullochs, to sell up and move south before they, too, were crushed, but by a sense of guilt. Overnight, Sarah Cowley had changed from a contented, hospitable woman to a bitter near-recluse, and her hostility extended to anyone who contrived for whatever purpose to deprive her of her son. It seemed to Kit that Mrs Cowley's whole personality had changed, casting an additional blight over Glenn's young life, but where his other friends were forced to turn away, frozen out and discouraged, Kit persisted for both of the Cowleys' sakes. There had been a time when Sarah Cowley had been very nice to her, and Kit was determined never to forget that. Grief was a terrible thing, and Sarah Cowley was taking longer than usual to adjust to her loss. What she needed was time. What Glenn needed was his friends to draw him out. Kit intended to persuade him to join the group that night, but first of all she would have to beg him for his help. The van had a bad habit of breaking down of late, and she would have to run in to Montville for additional supplies. She had absolutely no intention of being found wanting as far as Thorne Stratton was concerned, and not for the first time lately she would have to call on Glenn's support.

The private road leading to the property was an extravagance of trees. They spread their great branches so that they interlocked overhead, forming a continuous golden-green canopy that the sunshine pierced only lightly. It was magnificent country and the farm was lush with tropical produce: pawpaws, pineapples, mangoes, bananas and an increasing number of introduced exotics. A small glistening stream ran through the property, and Kit had to drive over a rickety wooden bridge before she came to the main gates. Two wonderful old banyan trees stood sentinel, and she saluted them lightly as she hopped out to open up. She should have rung, really, to check whether Glenn was home, but she did so dread Mrs Cowley's answering the phone. She sounded so cold and lifeless, it was like ringing the morgue, but as soon as the dismal thought sprang to mind, Kit cast it out. She, too, remembered very vividly the grief and shock of that terrible day, and her heart ached for Glenn's mother. If only Mrs Cowley wouldn't shut everyone out—so many good people wanting to help, so many with past experiences of coping with grief. But Sarah Cowley preferred to suffer alone, dissociating herself from the people and affairs of the district. There was an even more disturbing side to her neurosis, because not only had she withdrawn into isolation, but she was alienating her son. In adolescence, multiple roles had been thrust on Glenn. He was much more than an only son, he was his mother's whole existence, and the burden was already shaping his adult identity. Kit was his best friend, and sometimes, she thought anxiously, his only friend. And Glenn was a boy who had been popular and outgoing.

Two magnificent golden Labradors came pelting down the track, and Kit laughed with sheer pleasure as they leapt up to give her a warm welcome. She loved animals, had always begged for a pet, but Clare had persistently refused to have a dog or a cat in the house.

'They're more trouble than children,' she had often maintained, and Kit had been forced to accept the way her mother felt. When she had a home of her own, she

was determined to live her own way. Even poor Mrs
Cowley derived comfort from the dogs.

The Cowley farmhouse was little more than a cottage
built in the tropical vernacular, with surrounding verandas providing deep shade for the central core. The
simple timber columns and veranda balustrades were totally obscured by a brilliantly flowering cerise bougainvillaea, and Kit touched the papery flowers lightly as she
ran up the steps. The dogs had gone before her, and Mrs
Cowley, wearing an apron over a faded dress, walked
out on to the veranda, using the hem of the apron to
wipe flour from her hands.

'Oh, it's you, Kit,' she said in a voice totally without
expression.

'How are you, Mrs Cowley?' Kit asked with delib
erate breeziness.

'I'm well, Kit—and you?'

'Fine. Just fine.' Kit smiled and fingered a spray of
flowers. 'Doesn't the bougainvillaea make a magnificent
display?'

It should have been a safe topic, but Sarah Cowley
looked pained. 'I planted it when I was first married,'
she told Kit bleakly. 'At least *something* has survived.'

Kit bit her lip, meaning not to say anything, but as
usual words spilled out. 'But the spirit survives?' she
asked with deep sincerity. 'Loved ones don't lose their
identity because they're no longer with us; they live on
in the mind. You must have lots of wonderful memories,
Mrs Cowley?'

Sarah Cowley swung away violently, making a distressed sound. 'Except it's not memories I need, Kit. I
know you're a good girl, you mean well, but I'd like
you to remember you know nothing of life. That will
come later.'

'Forgive me, Mrs Cowley,' Kit apologised, following
her up. 'I never meant to hurt you.'

'It's not pleasant to be taken to task by a young girl.'

'That wasn't intended at all,' Kit said in some dismay.
'I'm young, I know, but I'm still capable of com-

passion. I feel for you very much, Mrs Cowley. You and Glenn.'

'Ah, yes, Glenn.' Sarah Cowley sat down abruptly and gave Kit an odd look. 'He's been a good friend to you, my son?'

'He has,' Kit agreed vigorously, the sun shafting through her riotously curling russet head, 'and I hope he has a good friend in me.'

'You've come to see him today, of course?'

'I've come to see you both,' Kit answered diplomatically.

The older woman almost sneered. 'We both know that's not true, Kit. You've been taking up a lot of Glenn's time, lately, with this and that. You really can't come running to him for every little thing. I suppose the van is playing up again?'

'As a matter of fact, it is,' Kit admitted wryly. 'I was hoping Glenn might be able to run me into Montville one day this week. An unexpected demand for supplies I haven't got. Of course, I'll pay him for the petrol.'

'You didn't before.'

Kit flushed. 'Because Glenn wouldn't take anything from me,' she protested quietly. 'Shall I give the petrol money to you?'

'Surely your father can fix the van?' Sarah Cowley suggested pointedly.

'I'm sorry to say he can't. Patrick has no mechanical bent. Even Glenn has nearly given up on it. What we really need is a new van, but it's way down the list of priorities.'

'So, meantime, you rely on my son's affection for you?' Sarah Cowley said baldly.

'I don't think it hurts anyone to do a good turn. Of course, I won't take up Glenn's time if you need him, but he does go into Montville for the farm.'

'And you thought you'd kill two birds with one stone?'

'Please don't see it like that, Mrs Cowley,' begged Kit.

'Except, of course, I do.' Sarah Cowley looked down at her tightly folded hands. 'I don't dislike you, Kit: I admire you. You exemplify so many of the lost virtues.

You're loving, loyal, respectful. I know you have a runaway tongue, but there's no hint of malice or mean-mindedness in you. You're amazingly beautiful, yet you're completely unaware of it. Your family are living the good life precisely because you started the gallery. It wouldn't have occurred to any of them without your direction. Your mother dotes on Melanie, who lags behind you in every way, yet you don't know the meaning of jealousy. You have everything going for you to make a real woman, but you *can't* have my son.'

'But, Mrs Cowley——' Kit, who had been leaning on the balustrade, jumped away in anxiety and shock.

'Do you know what it feels like, Kit, to be left alone?'

'In a sense, I do.' Kit collapsed into a nearby chair and grasped the older woman's unresisting hand. 'I'm nineteen years old, Mrs Cowley. Glenn is my friend. I don't want anybody. Your fears of any involvement are completely misplaced. Glenn and I are two friends who like and understand each other.'

'Is that what you *really* think, Kit?'

Kit stared back into the lack-lustre hazel eyes. 'Of course I do.'

'But you can't go back to being children again. Glenn lost a great deal when his father was killed, and his very lack has compounded his feeling for you. You're no ordinary girl. Other girls he grew up with could never measure up. It's not just your looks, it's your substance. With a girl like you, a man can make plans. I was vital, once.'

'I remember.'

'I can't be again, sad to say, Kit.'

'And too soon to say, Mrs Cowley,' said Kit earnestly. 'Please don't think me presumptuous, but you need time. Life won't always seem so intolerable. It should be hopeful.'

'Ah, Kit, you're so young, and every day your power grows. On the one hand, I like you, I've watched you grow. On the other I can't stand by and allow you to consume my son. He lives to help you—serve you, more like it. You've always taken hold of his imagination. Is it typical, do you suppose, to have a dolphin for a friend? Who else in the cove would Oskar accept? It's quite extraordinary—you have so much awareness, it crosses over boundaries. I believe your friendship with my son has already exceeded the point where it's safe for him.'

'All this because I ask the occasional favour?' Kit cried, amazed. 'I *do* them, Mrs Cowley.'

'I know you do, Kit, but you're missing my point. In all fairness, I expect you don't even see it. Glenn is in love with you.'

'Of course he isn't!' snorted Kit.

'My dear girl, do you want me to provide examples of his deep feelings?' Sarah Cowley returned harshly.

'When he's with me, he's happy, he's relaxed.'

'He's excited and on his toes. Yours is not a soothing presence, Kit, not like your dolly sister. You've so much life in you, you crackle. Even your hair dances around you in flames. You're too much for Glenn, and you'll hurt him.'

'Never!' Kit protested.

'Not intentionally, but you'll do it just the same. My son has already suffered too much. You're very important to him, Kit—you must know that.'

'And I try to be.' One of the dogs, upset by the palpable tension, gave Kit a nudge, and she pulled its splendid head on to her lap. 'We're being honest with each other. The last thing I want to do is hurt you, but Glenn is lonely. He has you, of course, but he needs his *friends.*'

'Not romantic developments, though. Romances that can't go anywhere.'

'There's no romance between Glenn and me. I wouldn't lie to you. You've concocted it, somehow. I care about him as a person. I care about you.' Kit went on, 'Now that we've started this thing please let me tell you, Glenn's personality is changing. It has a great deal to do with your loss, I know, but he hasn't enough interests. It's work, work, work and no fun. It's too extreme. There should be a greater balance.'

'And *you* don't work?' asked Sarah with heavy irony. 'Personally, I believe it's the parents' role to provide support for the child, but you're the one in your family who's had to find a way of doing things. You have capacities, Kit, that haven't even begun to be explored. You do the work and your family takes the credit. You don't think all of us here at the Cove give Melly the credit for all the things *you* make? You're a better painter now than your father will ever be, but he doesn't want to know.'

'That's not true, Mrs Cowley,' Kit said quietly. 'My father and I are very close.'

'Of course you are,' Sarah Cowley agreed tensely, rising and brushing some non-existent crumbs from her apron. 'Please respect my apprehension, Kit. If Glenn came to love you, then lost you, it could destroy him.'

'Then make sure he's with other people,' Kit pleaded. 'You do see he's not getting out enough, mixing? Glenn used to be so popular. Nothing can alter his love for you, but you want him to marry, don't you?'

'I look forward to the day, Kit. But not to you.'

'This is absolute nonsense!' Kit burst out in her spirited fashion. 'But why ever not? What's *wrong* with me?'

Sarah Cowley looked at her, thin face solemn. 'There's nothing wrong with you, Kit. I'm sure you'll bring some man great happiness, but I can simply say it as I see it. There's too much to you for Glenn. You'll move away from here, Kit, I know it. You're chafing now against the confines of your life. As you get older, you'll want so much more, and Glenn could never provide it. He's a simple farmer, like his father. I see this very clearly.'

'Dear, oh, dear...' Kit raised distressed violet-blue eyes. 'Has Glenn spoken to you about this?'

'Not a word.' Sarah's gaze was compelling in her thin, unmade-up face. 'I'm his mother, Kit. When you're a mother, you'll know.'

She turned and walked back into the house, and Kit remained where she was for a few moments, too stunned to move. All she knew of Glenn was that he had a deep affection for her, as she had for him. For years, she had

helped him with his homework. He had always carried
her satchel. They were devoted friends with a shared
background. Now Mrs Cowley was speaking of some
desperate ill-advised attachment. Poor wretched woman!

Kit stood up, determined not to make a fuss. ''I'll be
going now, Mrs Cowley,' she called through the door.

'Don't—Glenn will see you. He's on his way back to
the house.'

'Am I not to ask him to help me?'

'I'd be glad if you didn't, Kit.'

'All right, then.' Kit felt completely drained. 'I'll say
hello and go.' She walked down the steps to the van but,
before she had a chance to get in, the farm jeep swept
around the side of the house and braked in a swirl of
volcanic dust.

'Kit!' Glenn, slim, muscular, compact, slid from
behind the wheel, his attractive sun-tanned face creased
into a radiant smile. 'I think of you and you appear.'

'How goes it?' She threw back her head and met his
smiling hazel eyes.

'Hot, bruised, aching, what does it matter?' He bent
and gave her a real kiss on the cheek. 'How are things
at the store?'

'Picking up,' she remarked wryly. 'I had quite a big
order this morning from our latest arrival.'

'Not Thorne Stratton?' he jeered triumphantly.

'How did you know he was here?' Kit demanded.

'How, indeed!' Glenn put out his hand. 'Someone told
Sam. It's big news. Come up and have a cold drink with
me.'

'I really should be going, Glenn,' Kit protested.

'You came out here, didn't you?' he asked. 'If you're
going to be needing more supplies, I'm going into Montville on Friday. We could have lunch in town.'

'I don't know, Glenn,' she said in a quick voice.

'Don't be silly. You love the ride.' He stood at the top
of the steps, calling out to his mother. 'Mum, could I
have a beer? Kit will have a Coke. Sit down, Kit.' His
smooth-skinned face was shining. 'You look great—but
then you always do.'

There was a pause, then Mrs Cowley walked back on to the veranda with a laden tray. Kit looked up at her a little warily, but Sarah only had eyes for her son.

'Kit and I had a little talk a short time ago,' she told him.

'Great! It's lovely you're here, Kit.' Glenn swiftly downed his beer. 'Didn't even touch the sides! I don't like you driving the van, it could break down. It's as good as finished, you know. Look at the way the rust has eaten into the body.'

'I know, it's a terrible hulk.' Kit sipped at the Coke she didn't want.

'I'm filthy,' said Glenn, and looked down at his khaki work clothes. 'And you look a dream! What say we have dinner out tonight?'

'I've promised the others I'll see them at the hideaway,' Kit excused herself, knowing Mrs Cowley was watching her narrowly.

'So we'll join them there. I can't handle this dull life. I need a break.' He turned his head and spoke to his mother. 'You don't mind, do you, Mum?'

'Of course I don't, son.'

'You're the one who really needs a holiday,' he burst out feelingly. 'Why don't you go to Aunt Judy? She's always begging you.'

'And who would look after you?'

'Kit will,' Glenn smiled. 'She's not a bad cook.'

'*Good* cook,' corrected Kit.

Sarah Cowley stiffened. 'I'd go mad at Judy's. She'd marry me off again, given half a chance.'

'Well, this has been nice,' Kit murmured, and stood up purposefully.

'What time shall I call for you?' Glenn ruffled a hand through his curly brown hair. 'Just the thought of a night out has picked me up.'

Darn right, Kit thought.

'We're meeting around seven,' she informed him. 'Roslyn will be there.'

'I heard she was visiting.' Glenn rubbed his square chin.

'City life doesn't suit her, so she told me over the phone. She particularly asked about you.'

'Did she now? She's nice, Ros,' Glenn remarked casually, 'but she's not you. Now, I'm going to shower, shave and dress up in style.'

CHAPTER THREE

BY THE WEEKEND, everyone in Eden Cove and for miles around knew of the celebrity in their midst.

'Wow!' one of Kit's girl friends said to her. 'How much do you want for me to take your place at the party?'

Kit, to her surprise, realised *she* wanted to go. In whatever capacity.

She had seriously considered all that Mrs Cowley had said to her, and came to the conclusion that Mrs Cowley's fears concerning her relationship with Glenn were excessive, and largely a result of Sarah's own insecurities. Kit was convinced she was threatening no one. Glenn needed the companionship of his own age group, and Mrs Cowley would have to recognise the fact. It was a pain in the neck if hostilities should arise, but it seemed to Kit that her first priority was her friend. She could dissociate herself from Glenn and earn his mother's approval. But what about Glenn? Why should he be the victim of his mother's sense of rivalry, resentment, whatever the heck it was? Her friendship with Glenn was conspicuous for its warm, platonic feelings. They were almost like cousins. *Were?* It was true they were no longer children, but Kit felt confident their friendship should be sustained, no matter what.

Glenn had taken her into Montville on the Friday morning, helped her take on the extra supplies, and even ran her up to the beach house where Ben Russell, the caretaker, had unloaded the bulk order and carried it into the kitchen. Kit decided the whole thing had been worth her while. She had few big customers, and she could do with the extra money.

'What's he like, this Stratton guy?' Glenn had asked, to which Kit had shortly replied, 'Powerful.'

* * *

'What are you going to do with your hair?' Melly demanded on the Saturday evening, as Kit was dressing.

'I have great plans for it! Don't be silly, Melly. I'm going as the help, not as a guest.'

'I was only thinking, like Mummy, you'd better tone yourself down,' Melly said critically.

'How? Puffing powder all over my hair? Honestly, if I wasn't so well balanced, you and Mum would give me a complex. Tone myself down, indeed! Anyone would think there was something frightful about red hair!'

'Don't get mad,' Melly said soothingly. 'I bet you could hold your own with any of his guests. Some of them arrived by helicopter, did you know?'

'Mmm! I expect they're from the islands. There's going to be a big buffet in the dining-room. Mrs Russell wants me to be up there by six. Six to twelve—a nice little evening's work.'

Melly handed her the belt of her black skirt. 'Isn't it funny you're so much taller, yet you have a smaller waist?'

Kit shot her a smiling look. 'Well, for one thing, I get lots of exercise.'

'Oh, exercise!' Melly rolled over on the bed. 'I hate it. I never stand where I can sit. Actually, I like to lie down. How long is it since Mrs Cowley had her fangs into you?'

'I beg your pardon?' Kit swung around, startled. 'That's the craziest thing I've ever heard!'

'The few times we've seen her lately, she's been sort of sarcastic. I think she's terrified Glenn will want to marry you,' Melly explained.

'Yes, I think she is, poor woman. God knows why!' Kit looked uncomfortable.

Melly threw her head up, a look of deep amusement in her eyes. 'Glen is nuts about you.'

'A good thing he's been keeping it to himself.'

'I'm serious, Kit. Glenn sees no one but you.'

'Then it's a big mistake. Marriage is a long way off for us both. Years, I should think!'

'I can't wait to get married,' Melly remarked dreamily.

'Then you'd better learn to cook and tidy up. Little
things like that become increasingly important. Gosh,
it's difficult to make curly hair behave! How I wish I
had your satin locks, Melly! I'll have to tie it back with
a ribbon.'

'Good idea!' Melly hopped up. 'What about violet,
like your eyes? Do you think you should have worn a
satin blouse? Everything you wear looks so positive.'

'I like to make a statement.' Kit adjusted the soft
lapels. The deep cut of the V *was* a bit low. Clare would
no doubt tell her to find a pin. 'Don't bother with the
ribbon, Melly. I have a stiff black bow.'

Senator Gower's isolated northern retreat was perched
on one of the highest hilltops for miles along the sun-
drenched coastline. Built on three levels into the rock-
ribbed cliffs, it commanded incomparable views of the
succession of virgin bays, the colour-shot sapphire sea
and the maze of coral islets beyond.

The Senator himself was rarely there, but when he did
arrive he was usually accompanied by an entourage of
guests and staff, who invariably provided the Cove with
a lot of vicarious excitement. The Senator, over the past
few years, had even introduced a huge beach party for
all the locals, who didn't exactly return his hospitality
by mostly voting for the Opposition. Thorne Stratton
was not the first celebrity to have taken up residence.
Several others, tycoons, politicians, socialites, an
American film star addicted to big game fishing the
Barrier Reef, had been handed the keys over the past
year or so. Eden Cove was used to the comings and
goings of such glamorous folk, but Thorne Stratton was
more astonishing than most. Here was the pride of the
media world—a man with an international reputation
and the survivor of countless death-dealing assign-
ments. A hero, no less.

Trust me to recognise greatness, Kit mused as she drove
along the lonely beach road. Patrick had wanted to drop
her off—the family was dining with friends at Paradise
Point—but that left her with no way to get home. Pa-

:trick had suggested he would come for her afterwards,
but Clare had intervened, saying it would spoil their
evening, having to watch the clock. The van was perfectly capable of covering the short distance to the
headland.

Kit had not protested. Clare would never have taken
her eye *off* the clock for Melly. Melly was the centre of
their mother's life. Kit couldn't remember a time when
it had been different. Clare seemed compelled to treat
Kit as an outsider and, while Patrick made it clear these
disturbances upset him, peace was the essence of his
existence. It seemed he had sacrificed everything in order
to achieve it.

Sunset was majestic. Kit responded to the beauties of
nature at her deepest level. One day, she would paint a
tropical sunset just the way it was—if she lived so long!
Thorne Stratton and his guests would have a marvellous
view from the Beach House. Kit had never been inside,
she was too much of a nonentity for that, but she had
gained considerable familiarity with it from the water.
The front façade was nearly all glass, within a handsome
cedar frame, so the glorious dawns and sunsets would
fill all the major rooms.

Unaccountably, she was just a bit nervous about tonight. Normally, helping Mrs Russell would have been
a piece of cake, but Thorne Stratton's guests wouldn't
be friendly locals. They were the sort of people who
landed on lawns in helicopters, aliens from the heady
world of politics, business and society, and sometimes
such people could be incredibly self-important. It occurred to Kit that she didn't know if he was married.
He didn't *look* married. He looked dauntingly self-
sufficient. Just the sort of man to attract women in
droves.

Her not unpleasant speculations were interrupted by
the van's desperate cough.

'Go, damn you!' she gritted. 'Don't let me down now.'
She concentrated diligently on the road ahead, as though
she could accomplish miracles with her mind. It sud-

denly struck her how very much she was on her own.
'Why *me*?' she actually cried.

The coughs and sputterings developed into a veritable
paroxysm, and Kit pulled over to the side of the road.
This wasn't the first time such a thing had happened.
She had come to think of the van as nearly human, and
it did manage to behave like an elderly lady pushed
beyond her limits. She was going to have to get herself
a car, no matter what friction that proposal engendered.
Instead of handing over so much to the household, she
would have to keep more for herself, and that included
more of the gallery's profits. It was all very well to offer
her various talents, but she didn't have to come quite so
cheaply, she decided. Those shell bouquets, in particular, took a surprising amount of time, let alone the
sacrifice of her fingernails. She wondered why the willing
worker was frequently put upon.

The flame was already leaving the sky. There would
be a brief flush of mauve, then night would set in. Kit
had allowed extra time for the predictable fits and starts
of the van. She played a patient tattoo on the wheel,
then she restarted the ignition.

'Good girl!' The engine fired obligingly, then decided
it needed a bit of a lie-down. 'Dear God, I don't believe
this!' Kit moaned. But of course she did. A feature of
life was its absolute predictability. If one particularly
wanted to impress, something always cropped up to
cramp one's style. She would have to walk. It would
make an amusing little anecdote for Mrs Russell.

Kit locked the van—what for? she wondered smil-
ingly—and started off. Her experience of the van required that she was always equipped with a stout pair
of walking shoes, and good-humouredly she got into
stride. Ordinarily, she didn't mind a walk, but it was
growing late. Maybe someone from the house would look
out and see her but, if they were going to do it, it would
have to be now. Birds, in solid bands of emerald, indigo
and rose, were passing over her head at about twenty
feet, making for the trees. It struck her she was getting
thin; her waistband was loose.

After several minutes of brisk walking her skin was flushed with heat, her hair was escaping from its confines in damp, springy curls and her breath was whistling in her throat. In a book or a film, help was just about due to arrive, some kindly soul like a farmer with a wonderfully good face and a litter of pigs on board. Kit felt a flash of panic. A man like Thorne Stratton would be very demanding. She had intended to make an impressive début as the hired help, but obstacles were everywhere in these confusing days. It was one of her most telling characteristics that she always rose to a challenge.

When a car horn honked some distance behind her, Kit swung around, beaming. But that was as far as she got. Even in the failing light, she could see the long-haired hippie behind the wheel of an old Dodge Charger, a male companion hunched beside him. Kit had never seen them or the car before, which meant they were drifters passing through a million wild acres. It wasn't Kit's way to panic, but she could feel the muscles of her stomach give a sick clench.

'Hi!' the driver shouted, cruising up beside her.

'Good evening.' Kit's fine, pearly teeth almost snapped together. She kept a pleasant expression on her face, but without an encouragement.

'Seems like you broke down? That your van back there?'

She stared back at him with deliberate unconcern. 'It is. I'm making for friends—*Senator Gower's* place, up there.'

The hippy cut in briskly, 'What do you say? Hop in, grab a seat.'

'No worries,' Kit told him serenely. 'They've sent someone for me.'

'And just how did they do that?' he demanded with a mirthless laugh.

'Easy. They were watching for me.'

'Oh, yeah!' the companion, a lank-haired individual with a ridiculous, Mexican-type moustache, suddenly challenged in a rough, strangled voice.

'What worries me, they might think you're bothering me,' she told them curtly.

'Not good enough for yah, eh?'

Kit felt the heat of anger rush into her face. 'If I were you,' she said ominously, 'I'd take off.'

'Yes, ma'am!' the hippie mocked her, and his companion gave a half-witted giggle. 'Why don't you bring a little joy into our lives? My buddy here is bored.'

In one corner of her mind Kit felt fear, but she kept it under control. 'If you had any decency, you'd leave me alone. No one should be stupid enough to tangle with the Senator's guests.'

'*Guest*, in a get-up like that? Not that it would make any difference which way you was dressed up. You're one hell of a bird!'

The world was suddenly shrouded in danger, and Kit increased her pace, not daring to look sideways at that leering face. The position of women in a male-dominated world could be hateful. She was bursting with the need to do something, but she didn't know what to do. Pity she didn't have a small hand-gun to pull from her bag! These two were surely without scruples.

Head down, moving vigorously, Kit failed to see what the moustachioed individual did. 'Ain't that a Jag comin' down the track?' he shouted in a voice that bored through Kit's skull.

'You bet your life it is,' gritted Kit, almost light-headed with relief.

'I don't know I'm frightened of some old geezer in a Jag,' the hippie observed, rubbing one eye socket.

'You will be once you see him!' Kit cried sharply.

'Let's take off, Denny,' the moustachioed one urged.

'No, man.' The hippie's face was set. 'Let's stick around and see what happens. What's a silly old sod in a flash car? What are we doin', anyway? Just cruising along.'

'I might claim you were harassing me,' Kit warned him. 'Do what your friend says—take off.'

'—— you, lady.'

The Jaguar ate up the road. It took about two minutes, in all. Its main beam came on as Kit charged to the back of the Dodge, and from there to the opposite side of the road. The car lunged to a stop and Thorne Stratton leapt out, calling to her in a voice that crackled with hard urgency.

'Miss Lacey!'

She might have been a Victorian maiden. She could have swooned at his feet, but instead she all but went into his outstretched arms. 'Thank God you arrived!' she gasped.

'You're OK, aren't you?' he cracked out.

'I'm OK. Let's get out of here.'

'I'm calling the shots.' Thorne bundled her into the car and slammed the door.

'Mr Stratton!' Kit tried to wind the window down, but there was only a series of switches on the centre console.

By this time, Thorne Stratton had crossed the road and was leaning in the passenger window of the now stationary Dodge.

'What the heck——' The switches controlled nothing; the ignition was off.

Kit opened the door, preparing to jump out, but as she did so Throne Stratton turned and barked out, 'Stay in the car!'

Spunky as she was, she lacked the courage to ask why.

He looked as powerful and arrogant as the devil himself. The hippies appeared to have folded down like a pack of cards; the moustachioed one even had a protective hand over his eyes.

'Oh, what it is to be a man!' Kit muttered to herself vehemently. For a few moments there, she had experienced a peculiar feeling of helplessness. She was Woman, a natural victim, and she had hated the feeling.

Finally, Thorne Stratton straightened up, rapped the hood of the Dodge, and it went into a U-turn and sped off.

'My hero!' Kit applauded him with burning blue eyes.

He didn't respond with a smile. He slid into the driving seat, hollow-cheeked and iron-jawed.

'I suppose you told them to get lost?'

'I told them,' he said harshly, 'to be well clear of this community in under an hour. I'll get the police to hurry them along.'

'They weren't actually *doing* anything,' Kit protested faintly.

'How can you be so foolish?' he demanded curtly, switching on the engine.

'How do you mean?'

'Don't big-eye me. I've encountered you exactly three times, and on two occasions you've been doing something positively dangerous.'

'Surely it isn't all that dangerous to break down?' Kit put up her hands to restore order to her hair. 'I couldn't help it.'

'I think you *can*,' he contradicted.

'Look, take it easy!' she cautioned him spiritedly.

'I've got a lot more to say to you. What do you suppose could have happened to you if I hadn't shown up? Another rape for the morning papers?'

'Never mind. You saved me!'

'Don't be flip with me, young lady.'

'So it was a sticky moment!' He seemed so angry, she actually tried to placate him. 'It's never happened before—I know everyone for miles around.'

He shot her a golden, contemptuous look. 'Most crimes are committed by someone known to the victim. That van of yours is only good for the demolition yard.'

'I've got feelings,' Kit said wryly.

'Those idiots were far from finished with you.'

'I know that.' Dutifully, Kit hung her glowing head.

'You can thank your lucky stars I was on the look-out for you,' he continued.

'I do—I will.'

'All that bravado is just a cover. I could feel the tremble right through your body.'

Kit gave a shaky laugh. 'It wasn't as bad as it probably looked.'

'Little fool!' he snapped.

Not even Patrick could have sounded so angry. 'You want to get rid of some of that hostility before you go back to your guests.'

'The hostility, Miss Lacey, is directed at you.'

'So what gives you the right?' demanded Kit.

'I'm passionate about preserving innocence, life.'

'I have a father to protect me!' she nearly shouted, the hot colour flying into her cheeks.

'Who lets you race about, after dark, in a wrecked van?'

'Don't you start on my father,' she warned him.

'And one more thing. What about your infatuated suitor? Couldn't he have run you up to the house? Surely he cares enough to offer?'

'He's not my suitor!' Kit felt angry, brilliant tears spring to her eyes. 'He's my friend. He comes from a very sober household. Not even a mild flirtation is allowed. Anyway, what has it to do with *you*? You've had a mind to make me over from day one.'

'You have all the ingredients for trouble.'

'So I've been told.'

Kit swept her glorious, unruly mane from her face. '*Who* told you?'

'My mother.' Kit's small fists were clenched. 'I think it has something to do with my flashy appearance.'

That apparently shook him, because he slowed the car to stare at her. 'Are you telling me that's the way your mother describes your looks?'

'Why not?' Kit gave him a quick look. 'It's the way she sees it. We all have ideals.'

'And parents have a way of vaunting their offspring.'

'So they do. My mother loves me, she just doesn't identify with my looks. I suppose it's because they're so very different from her own. A good many people claim to dislike red hair. I'll have to call it red.'

'The most striking shade of red I've even seen,' Thorne admitted drily. 'I think I could risk saying it's your glory. One usually doesn't have to call attention to physical beauty. Most beauties I've known have been incredibly self-centred.'

'Well, that lets me out.'

He glanced at her, and one eyebrow flared ever so slightly. 'Wasn't your mother anxious about you in that van?' he asked.

'Of course she was. I mean, the van can make it to the headland.'

'So no one foresaw that it could break down?'

'I've got walking shoes, haven't I?' she pointed out wryly. 'What's important for you to remember, as you're so angry, is that everyone knows me.'

Once more, the brilliant topaz gaze flickered in her direction. 'The reality of the situation is, you can't control who drifts in and out of your safe little world. The north's isolation is being rapidly replaced by a fast developing tourist industry. You know the increasing number of people who spend time in your gallery. Most men would mean you no harm, but those two were pretty much trash.'

'Close the door, Kit,' Mrs Russell said to her as she hurried into the kitchen. 'Some bitch of a woman has been barging in here, giving me orders.'

'You're upset.' Kit went to the older woman and pressed her well padded shoulder.

'Mr Stratton is such a gentleman,' Mrs Russell huffed. 'He gives me every respect and consideration.'

'I'm here now,' Kit said soothingly. 'Everything will be all right.'

'I don't know. She was so put out when he went after you. Waiting for you, he was. Watching to see you'd make it in your old van. His lady friend didn't like it one little bit. Anyone would think it was his wife! Seemed to think it was most unusual.'

'What's it got to do with her?' Kit asked.

'Well, she's been giving him lots of meaningful looks. Soon as you meet her you'll realise what she's like. Dear, oh, dear, look what I've done now!'

'Here, let me.' Kit looked over the lavish host of hors-d'oeuvres. 'I'll grab an apron. What delectable things you've thought up to give them!'

The housekeeper's flushed face lightened. 'You think so?'

'Everything looks superb. And what a house! Those great window walls! There's no barrier to the sea and the sky.'

They worked along swiftly and companionably; Kit, with her eye for colour and texture and taste, arranging the delicious little appetisers on large pottery platters.

'I've got lots of hot things as well,' Mrs Russell told her. 'In ten minutes or so, you'd better start taking things out.'

'About time!' the stunning blonde woman exclaimed as she swept through the closed door and gave Kit a severe up and down.

'Certainly, madam,' Kit responded with sardonic calm.

'One moment—what's your name?'

Kit's vivid face lit in a wry smile. 'Christiana,' she said impishly.

The fair eyebrows rose disbelievingly, and Kit was subjected to a piercing look. 'If you don't mind, I'd like the truth!' the woman snapped.

'I always speak the truth, madam.' Kit's good humour was threatened. 'Now, if you don't mind, I'd like to start serving. Mr Stratton has given precise instructions as to what he wants done.'

Behind her, Mrs Russell gave an uncontrollable gurgle that was quickly choked off, but the imperious blonde was not to be bested.

'I realise there might be problems getting suitable staff up here, but you're more insolent than most!' she said angrily.

'Forgive me, we've all been living a very quiet life.'

'I'll let Mr Stratton know,' the blonde answered darkly, and swept out of the door, leaving behind a mild shock and the lingering traces of her expensive perfume.

'*Told* you!' Mrs Russell poured herself a quick sherry and nearly upset the bottle. 'Thank God there aren't too many of her up here. And she's got the cheek to call *you* insolent. Why, you're a princess compared to her!'

The blonde's name, as Kit was soon to find out, was Alyce Schaffer. *The* Alyce Schaffer, born Pelham, daughter and widow of two extraordinarily affluent men, once roughly the same age.

One thing was certain, she had taken an instant and violent dislike to Kit.

'Sure I don't have another knife in my back?' Kit joked every time she came back into the kitchen. 'What have I ever done to her?'

'I expect you'll discover, one of these days,' Mrs Russell laughed. Kit had learned many things in her short lifetime, but she had never learned a simple truth: she was a genuine natural beauty, the rarest of all creatures, and beauty drew a disturbing amount of conflict.

One of Thorne Stratton's guests, a distinguished-looking man in his late fifties, appeared to glance at Kit often but, apart from thanking her courteously each time she served him, he said nothing. It had occurred to her that he was looking at her overmuch but, like Thorne Stratton, there was nothing remotely indelicate in his regard. For some reason she interested him, in the same way that Kit was interested in a work of art.

It was as Kit was leaving the kitchen with a tray of steaming hot coffees that Alyce Schaffer once more pushed in, and in doing so set the silver tray flying.

'Ooh!' Kit drew in her breath swiftly as the scalding coffee drenched her white blouse and seared her skin.

'Oh, my dear!' Mrs Russell snatched up a tea-towel.

'I'm sorry. It was an accident.' With a frown of disgust, Alyce Schaffer watched the coffee stains spread.

'Please,' Mrs Russell asked coolly, 'would you mind moving out of the way?'

'Now this has happened, you should go home.'

'I believe you did that deliberately!' Kit shot back. 'You've been timing me in and out of the door.'

The blonde's hand went to her exquisite pearl and diamond pendant. 'You should control yourself. You're an incredibly rude girl.'

'That must be hurting you, Kit?' Mrs Russell threw a quick, distressed look into Kit's eyes.

'It *was* hot!' Gingerly, Kit held her blouse away from her skin. 'I'll have to take this off.'

'Not here, if you don't mind,' snapped Alyce Schaffer.

'I'll speak to Mr Stratton. It should be all right.'

'Speak to me about what?' Thorne Stratton himself appeared in the open doorway, tall, elegant, faintly smiling. 'Damn it all, Kit, what's happened?' The smile quickly changed to a frown.

'Little accident with the coffee tray,' she shrugged. 'Nothing serious.'

'Serious enough to be hurting.'

'All's well, Thorne,' Alyce Schaffer drawled soothingly. 'I'll find something for the girl, and perhaps your caretaker could run her home. I'll serve the coffee myself.'

'Let's get some cream on you now,' Thorne Stratton said crisply, and took hold of Kit as though she were a child. 'That's very kind of you, Alyce. I only came in to tell you Judge Harrison takes his coffee black, not white.'

'Out-manoeuvred!' crowed Kit as she was being led away.

'What are you talking about?' He looked down at her from his superior height.

'You out-manoeuvred your lady friend.'

'She's *not* my lady friend. I don't expect you to involve yourself in my relationships.'

'Prying into *my* background I consider even worse!'

He led her down the long cool corridor of polished rain-forest timbers, and opened up a door to a spacious bedroom. 'Let's go into the en-suite bathroom.'

'You're awfully keen to play doctor,' she said suspiciously.

'All you have to do is hold your tongue.'

'Why? I'm not a child. We won't have a saner world unless women are allowed to talk.'

'There's no need to get hysterical.'

The bathroom was pure white except for an arched stained glass window reaching almost from floor to ceiling. Voluptuous green ferns and tropical orchids added an alluring splash of colour.

'Whatever am I going to put on?' Kit looked down at her sodden, ruined blouse.

'I've not decided as yet.' He had opened up a mirrored cupboard and was searching inside. 'Ah, this should do!' He selected a long, pale blue tube of cream.

'Many thanks.' Her hand came up to snatch it. Without her knowing why, her whole body had begun to tremble.

'A pity to damage such beautiful skin. You should check before you go charging through doors.'

'Especially when there's someone to be reckoned with on the other side.

He was looking down at her intently through half-closed lids. 'When you're ready, call out. I'll pass you one of my shirts.'

'Oh, fine.' Kit only allowed herself a brief glance. This man was appallingly dangerous to her, and already he knew it.

The hot liquid had left large red blotches on her neck, breast and midriff. She surveyed herself thoughtfully as she rubbed the soothing cream in. Her first brush with a bigger world and she had made herself an enemy. It was generally recognised that even the smartest man didn't know when a woman was making a play for him. Alyce Schaffer was displaying the classic symptoms of a jealous woman. Didn't she realise she had absolutely nothing to worry about? How would a man like Thorne Stratton be interested in someone he regarded as a mere teenager? As any sensible person would say, there was no contest, yet Kit was experienced enough to appreciate that the hostility was sexual.

'Everything OK?' A tap came at the door.

'Yes, I'm fine.' Kit opened the door a little and put her hand around it.

His laugh was light, brief, but explosive. 'Modesty matters.'

'You bet it does!' Kit rolled her wet bra inside her blouse and folded it down neatly. His shirt she could have wrapped around herself several times. Lean as he was, his shoulders were wide, and he was so tall. Finally she belted it and bloused out the fine burgundy cotton. There was a hectic flush in her cheeks—a dead giveaway, she thought.

'Very fetching!' he drawled.

'I wouldn't put it as flatteringly as that.'

'So I've already seen. I can't wait to meet the rest of your family.'

Alyce Schaffer was standing almost outside the door, her laugh both breathy and forced. 'Good heavens, Thorne, I could have managed to find something!' Her ice-blue eyes were as cold as arctic floes. 'If you go to the kitchen, dear, the caretaker has agreed to drive you home.'

'I suppose I am through for the night.' Kit glanced up at Thorne Stratton. 'I'm sorry I couldn't get to finish what I'm being paid for. I *am* being paid, I hope?'

His disturbing mouth twisted. 'I can't change our deal now. There's no need for Ben to get the car out—I'll run you back to your place. Alyce can play hostess while we're gone.'

'But your guests!' protested Alyce.

'Please excuse me,' Kit said quickly. 'I'll say good-night to Mrs Russell.' She could see the helpless fury in the other woman's eyes. Anyway, wasn't he being extra-ordinarily thoughtful? Ben *could* take her.

'Deliberate, it was,' Mrs Russell confirmed. 'She upset all that coffee on you so you'd have to leave.'

'Well, she's getting just what she wanted. I'm leaving now. Where's Ben?'

Thorne Stratton caught Kit up as she went in search of the caretaker.

'Where do you think *you're* going?' he demanded.

'Your *guests*!' she mimicked mockingly. 'The one thing I can't do is come between you and them.'

'It would be interesting to see how you develop,' he commented a little edgily. 'I dislike having my decisions changed.'

'Now that has a familiar ring. Most men do... Who was that man who was staring at me?' Kit asked as they drove away.

'Which man?' he murmured drily.

'Late fifties. Silver hair, moustache, nice voice.'

'Judge Harrison. I thought you knew.'

'I only recall a lot of Christian names. Every time I turned around, he was looking at me in the most curious way—as though he'd seen me before and he couldn't think where.'

'You have that effect on *me*,' said Thorne.

'Is that why you offered to drive me home?' Every inch of her was oddly on fire. He had a powerful ability to unsettle her, and she tried to banish it with flippancy.

'The sooner you're safely there, the better.'

His abruptness took her breath. 'I've no wish to be an imposition. Pull over and I'll walk.'

He ignored her. 'Where the hell's that van?'

'What?' She stared ahead, startled.

He switched the lights to main beam, but where the van should have been there was only darkness.

'Don't tell me someone towed it away?' Kit gasped.

'More likely those two morons turned around and came back. Stay in the car and I'll have a look around.' Thorne pulled over to the thickly grassed verge, but as he killed the engine and hopped out so did Kit.

'Don't you ever do what you're told?' he thundered.

'There it is. They've rolled it!' Impetuously, she broke away from him, running down the slope. The van was over on its side, apparently wedged against a stand of palms. The powerful lights from the Jaguar brought it clearly into view.

'For God's sake!' Thorne grabbed her, not caring in his urgency that the strength of his bear-hold almost cracked her ribs. '*Stand still*, you little fool!'

The hillside seemed to tilt, and while Kit staggered in disbelief he bore them both violently to the ground, shielding her with his own body. She heard the impotent rage in his oath, then the van rocked grotesquely and crashed down the slope. The explosion was deafening, and columns of orange-red flames instantly blazed against the darkness.

'My dear God!' It was a transfixing sight, and Kit panicked and, half crushed, gave a smothered wail. Her shock was chaotic, stampeding down her nerves so madly it was impossible to rein it in. There were answering tremors in Thorne's hard, lean body, and only then did she consider the terrible risk she had offered them both. It wasn't his first experience of burning vehicles; the Asian diplomat's car had burned while he had lain wounded for many hours in the wake of attack.

'I'm ashamed,' she whispered into the base of his throat.

'Forget it.'

'I can't. You're trembling.'

'The hell I am!' he said edgily. 'That's spontaneous radical reaction. I was a long time in hospital.'

'Hold on to me,' she invited.

'Crazy girl!' Even with the pungent heated fumes blowing over them in waves his voice lightened.

'All right, I accept it.' In the eerie crimson light, Kit could see his face quite clearly. 'You put yourself at risk for me.'

'Why shouldn't I?' Softly, very softly, he brushed grit from her cheek. 'From the little I've seen of you, I'm convinced you'd do the same for me. One thing, lady, you never, *never* race towards a rolled car. It's a wonder it didn't explode before this!'

'Do you know we've been acquainted for less than a week and I've dragged you down a hillside?' she said wryly.

'That qualifies you for my friendship, I'm sure.' He made no attempt to move, but watched the van burn.

'I've never met anyone remotely like you,' she remarked feelingly.

'You've never met *anyone*.'

'No need to sound so dismissive!' snapped Kit.

'You don't think so?' He sounded ironic. 'Together now, Miss Lacey, we'd better get up.'

'Can you believe it, I don't want to.' She turned her head and buried it in the crook of his arm.

'You're going to, little one.'

How had this happened? Was it some dark fantasy?

'Christiana,' he said warningly.

'I never knew how reassuring a man's presence could be,' she sighed.

'You're not cutting your eye-teeth on me. I've learnt to be cautious in all things.'

But Kit could not control her runaway excitement. I'm not a child, she thought. I'm a woman. A *woman*. This man is beautiful to me. Not only beautiful, a hero.

'No, Kit,' he said crisply, and pulled them into a sitting position.

'How old are you?' She turned her haloed head to stare into his face.

'Too old for a mere child.'

'I see no signs of age. You're a stunning-looking man.'

'Sure.' The brackets at the side of his sculptured mouth deepened. 'I'm not about to offer as your first affair.'

'No, no, I've had lots.' She made a less than efficient attempt to straighten his wrap-around shirt.

'And all the while a virgin. You're very beautiful, little one. You look great in my shirt, but you're a protected species as far as I'm concerned.'

'What a pity!' she sighed. 'I'd give anything to know what it's like being kissed by a glamorous international news correspondent.'

Thorne drew her a little roughly to her feet. 'For all your *élan*, you are *so* innocent.'

She tilted up her chin. 'What's it like to kiss Alyce Schaffer? I bet she didn't have to wait to find out.'

'Might I remind you that she's a sophisticated, mature woman?'

'In my opinion, she's a fair terror!'

He put a hard, guiding arm around her and compelled her up the hillside. 'She manages to hide it very successfully from me.'

'Then she must be two people, one for you and one for me. Have you ever been married?'

'Mercifully, not even once.'

'You have something against marriage?'

'Do you have to know?'

'I'm here,' she pointed out.

'Very much here. We'll have to ring the police again about this. The fools must be crazy if they think we can't catch them.'

'The van wasn't insured,' Kit told him.

'I didn't think it was. I think I owe you. Their spite was directed more at me than you.'

'My opinion exactly, but I couldn't bring myself to accept charity. You were telling me your life story.'

He shook his dark blond head.

'You're saying you weren't? I'm a good listener.'

Rather tautly, he gripped her arm. 'Get in the car, Kit, like a good girl.'

'Getting to you, aren't I?' she jeered.

'You might wish you weren't.'

'Why, are you dangerous?' She had been drawn to him from the very first minute, and she was only nineteen.

'The answer to that is obvious. I am, to *you*.'

'This has been a very exciting night,' Kit said tersely as she buckled herself into her seat. 'If you fancy you have a debt to me, I'll accept a chaste peck goodnight. Danger has brought us together, increased the pace.'

'Be still!' he ordered crossly.

'Who do you look like, your mother or your father? You have the most striking profile.'

'My mother,' he said brusquely, 'according to a lot of people. I'm my father inside.'

'Did something go terribly wrong?' she asked quietly.

He threw her a glittery look. 'I adored my mother. She left my father when I was eight years old. Both of us always looked on it as a massive defection, so when she wanted to come back we both said no.'

'How old were you when she wanted to come back?'

'Fourteen.' His voice turned sardonic. 'I don't understand why I'm telling you this.'

'You admire me, that's why. Where is your mother now?'

'She's always had a string of lovers. She was and is a very beautiful woman.'

'And your father?'

'My father is dead. He was a very highly placed diplomat, and my mother's betrayal went a long way to destroy him. Now, if you don't mind, I think our little chat is over.'

Kit put her head back. 'You know how to inflict a little hurt yourself.'

'You'd do well to remember it.'

CHAPTER FOUR

EXCEPT for the soft flooding of the lush, tropical garden, the house was in darkness when they arrived.

'Your parents not home yet?' Thorne demanded, stepping out of the car.

'I'm afraid my father doesn't go in for early nights,' Kit told him. 'He's a great one for company. He loves good food, good wine, good talk.'

'While you're at the mercy of a couple of thugs?'

Despite herself, Kit cringed a little. 'Wait a minute, Mr Stratton. I told you not to criticise my father.'

'What *should* I do?' he asked ironically.

For once, she refused the challenge. 'I love him,' she said quietly.

'That's fine for him.' There was a faint trace of anger in his beautiful, well bred voice. 'I'll see you safely into the house.'

'That's kind of you,' Kit responded with half-mocking thanks. 'Would you care to come in for a few moments or am I keeping you from your guests?'

'That depends what you mean by a few moments. I can't help wishing your parents were home. You didn't tell those two hippies your name, or where you lived?'

'Good grief, no!' She whirled and looked up at him, feeling a strange excitement like needles piercing her skin. 'You're looking at one smart girl.'

'And enormously popular, so I hear.'

'I haven't a clue what you're talking about.'

'Of course you do. Glenn Cowley, isn't it? He'd give his life for you.'

'I don't think he's fond enough of me for that!'

'Mrs Russell seems to think so. She has a positive genius for gossip.'

'And for exaggeration.' Kit searched around the rim of a giant terracotta planter for the key, and as usual a thorn of the orange bougainvillaea stabbed her. 'Please come in.' She opened up the door and switched on the lights.

'Maybe this isn't such a good idea,' Thorne decided.

'Why ever not?' Her face was a pale cameo, framed by her abundant hair.

'For one thing, you're positively quivering with emotion.'

'But you're indifferent, aren't you?'

'Of course I am, Miss Lacey. Never doubt it.' He left her standing in the doorway and walked further down the short hallway. 'This is a very attractive house.'

'We like it.' She was pleased by the genuine interest in his voice. 'Patrick was the architect, builder. We had a few sub-contractors in—electricians, plumbers, that kind of thing. It only took six months to build. Of course, it's very simple in form, but it works. The emphasis is on the view. We used all local timbers, Queensland hardwoods, native walnut, cedar. The layout of the house was ideal to start a gallery.'

'*Your* idea?'

She shook her head. 'My father's. Most of the beautiful things you see around here are for sale.'

'Not you?'

Some shade of expression in his eyes filled her with confusion. 'All *I* do is run the store.'

He picked up a small bronze sculpture, smoothed it with his hands, then set it down again. 'According to Mrs Russell, you have exceptional artistic gifts.'

'I'm not even half as good as Mrs Russell thinks. She's watched me grow up, you know. Everything I do she regards with a fond eye. We *do* have some very gifted people showing here. A beautiful, peaceful environment is a major consideration for artists. It's a great pleasure for us to exhibit their work.'

'I'm sure it is!' His eyes moved slowly from object to object, lingering on one of Kit's floral arrangements of spreading foliage, dracena, strelitzia, large leaves of dieffenbachia set in one of Patrick's ceramic troughs, all foils for a spray of exquisite white orchids. 'Your work?'

'Actually, yes. I think it's rather good. When you have the time, I could show you more of the gallery.'

'I'd be delighted,' he returned suavely. 'I can see your father's work. Where is your own?'

'I panic about my own work. It's not good enough to be shown.'

'Why don't you let *me* be the judge of that? I grew up in a house full of collections. It was a tremendous feat not to knock into something, and it was a very large house. My paternal grandfather built up one of the finest collections of Oriental antiquities in the world. Apart from a dozen or so choice pieces, he bequeathed it all to the British Museum—the Keeper at that time was one of his close friends. My love affair with Asia began in my childhood. By the time I went to university I was familiar with most of her great cities, from Bangkok to Baghdad, Moscow to Manila.'

'And the languages, how did you get on about them?'

'It was awkward for a while. I had to provide myself with an MOL. It helped.'

Kit curled her hands around a chair. 'Care to explain the MOL?'

'Master of Oriental Languages.' Thorne bowed slightly, Mandarin fashion. 'You could say I cut my baby teeth on the Orient.'

'How marvellous!' she cried, an excited sparkle in her blue-violet eyes. 'I must seem very ordinary and ignorant to you.'

His amusement was obvious. 'Ordinary enough when I first saw you to take my breath away.'

'You're serious!' A lifetime of subtle brainwashing was reflected in her voice.

'My dear, I've never been able to pass a thing of beauty without staring at it,' he pointed out with smooth detachment. 'Now, I'll stay just long enough to pass judgement on your finest work. I'll bet you have a room full of them.'

Kit had to smile. 'Yes, since I started daubing when I was about two. You're an educated man. You won't hurt my feelings if you simply give me the straight truth. Or rather, it might hurt, but that's what I want.'

'I don't think anyone will ever accuse you of being a coward,' he said mildly. 'Off you go.'

Suddenly, she blossomed with confidence. For all Clare's spreading influence, she clung to the belief in her own gifts. All her life she had been trying to unburden her soul to someone. But why *now*, to this dangerous man?

In her bedroom she did an uncharacteristic thing—darting to her mirror to check her appearance. She thought she looked a clown in his oversized shirt. Her face was dominated by her eyes. They were hectically brilliant, suggesting her inner turmoil. Her cheeks were flushed and her full cushioned mouth was too soft and eager. Even her body was at the mercy of her feelings, because her nipples peaked against the fine burgundy cotton. She was a sight to horrify her mother: a young girl drenched in sexual radiance.

'Keep cool, Kit,' she urged herself. 'Keep cool.'

Two of her most recent works were stacked against the wall, gouache and watercolours. Her friends Milt and Robyn Edwards, the artists, had done a superb job of framing them. Kit scooped them up quickly and carried them back into the long gallery. Strange, she didn't dread showing them, even when she knew Thorne was a man of considerable cultural authority.

'For the past year I've been dabbling in fantasy,' she explained briefly, positioning the paintings automatically in the best light. 'It all started when some friends of ours brought back some hanging scrolls from Japan. Of course, they were exquisite and they gave me inspiration. There's nothing new under the sun.'

'But new ways of saying it.' He came to stand directly behind her, an impassive face but keen, evaluating eyes.

The first painting showed two gorgeous tropical parrots, predominantly of a rich red, perched amid the long silky leaves of a rain-forest tree. Kit had treated it

in the traditional manner, as a totally authentic illus-
tration, but the second was pure fantasy, as improbable
as a dream, but drawing on the arresting beauty and
mystery of a tropical Eden. The shadowy female figure
was herself lost in a sensual enchantment; birds, trees,
flowers, more voluptuous than life. While she had
painted it, her head had been full of crushed jewels, and
it seemed to her now this was how it appeared.

'Flamboyant, Kit, just like yourself,' Clare had commented when she had seen it. Clare, the expert. Clare
had never approved of Kit's imaginary life, even the
games she had played as a child. Kit was *too* different.

'Well?' She looked up at him, injecting a certain
breathlessness in her manner. Even under a brilliant light
which burnished the dull gold of his hair his face was
full of shadows, temples, cheekbones, scooped-out
hollows down to the dent in his chin. To the imaginative
Kit, always ready for flight of fancy, he looked like some
golden god. Not the playful, benevolent kind, but the
kind where imperiousness counted for a lot. His
expression gave nothing away.

'Go on, tell me,' she said. 'Nothing would surprise
me.'

'My dear child,' he said finally.

'Go on. That's not enough to live on.' She actually
clutched his arm.

'These are quite astonishingly beautiful.'

Instead of flushing, she lost all colour. 'Re-e-a-lly?'
It was almost a stutter.

'That flowerlike human creature is yourself?'

'I'm not afraid of painting myself nearly nude,' she
explained.

'What are you going to do with it?'

'Hang it in the privacy of my bedroom. The parrots
are for sale. Lots of people love my birds.'

'So, no difficulty there?' He turned slightly to stare
down at her.

'We sell Patrick's and our other artists' first. I have
heard my colours are over-rich.'

'I wish whoever told you knew what they were talking about. This fantasy here could be the set for some marvellous ballet. You're familiar with the great watercolours of the theatre, I suppose? Benois, Bakst and the great painters that came after?'

'Unfortunately, no,' she murmured apologetically, then rallied, 'There's so much I want to know, so much I have to learn. I'm full of hopes and dreams. I don't quite know why. I've been like it since a child.'

'Genuine artists always are,' he told her drily. 'It's wrong to keep you wrapped away. You should be catching up with your education.'

'Education costs money,' Kit pointed out.

'In the meantime, libraries are usually a rich source of information.'

'The nearest is twenty-six miles away, and you know the sad story of the van. Did it *really* blow up, or am I dreaming all this?'

'It blew up, all right,' Thorne replied harshly, a look of threat in his topaz eyes. 'They might regard themselves well away, but they'll be caught. Are these for sale?'

'Sale?' she repeated blankly.

'I'm not being kind.''

'Of course you're not. You're not kind. I knew from the moment I laid eyes on you, you're a very daunting man.'

'I suppose that's why you spoke to me so tartly?'

'I'm a staunch feminist.'

'No one's perfect. What you've got here, Christiana, is quite exceptional. For anywhere. The parrots are startlingly good, but I'm more interested in your dreams. Watercolor, though one of my favourite media, can be appallingly prosaic, but you've used a whole range of jewel colours that work beautifully. It's incredibly sensuous. Properly managed, you could be a considerable success. I envy you such a gift.'

Though Kit couldn't wrench her eyes from his face, she couldn't speak.

'Lost your tongue?' drawled Thorne.

A shadow passed over her bemused expression. 'You wouldn't lie to me.'

'Drop the false modesty, little one. You know you're good.'

'I know less than you think,' she answered him.

'You know how to use your eyes. Surely your family have offered you the greatest encouragement?'

'Of course,' she lied blithely. 'I have plans, Thorne Stratton. I'm not going to be a nobody all my life.'

'My dear,' he bowed sardonically, 'you *couldn't* be a nobody, if only because of that hair. I've never seen such contrasts in colouring—a redhead with golden skin and black eyebrows and lashes. I expect it runs in the family?'

'That's the worst of it, I'm not like anyone!'

'No one has your eyes? They're a singular colour.'

'Morning Glory,' Kit smiled, her whole expression soft with affection. 'That's the term Patrick uses. Now, if you want to see a *really* masterly painting, you should see Patrick's portrait of Melly and me. It's his master-piece, but would you believe he's never painted a por-trait before or since? Except one, and he said he destroyed it. I know he never did.'

'And how is that?' he demanded, as though he would really like to know.

'Good gracious, I know my own father!'

'I'd like to meet him.'

'That's easily seen to. Patrick loves people. Especially clever people.'

'And he lives here? Forgive me, I know it's extremely beautiful, but far too easy-going and undemanding for real life.'

This was so much what Kit often thought, her flow of words dried up. 'It's a family secret, I think,' she finally managed facetiously, yet there was a hint of sadness and perplexity in her eyes. 'What makes people act as they do? I can't solve the enigma that's my father. Sometimes I think our whole life is play-acting, that none of us are really what we think we are. According to my father, he took refuge from a mad world. Lots of people do. This is only a small colony, but you've only to look around you to see the wealth of talent.'

'All of whom you contrive to reduce to the mundane.' An expression of something approaching disgust crossed his handsome, chiselled features. 'I could put you in touch with a dozen people right now. I don't think I'll do it, however. You're not ready. Obviously, you know nothing of the world. I believe you're not even aware of your own ability. I propose to pay you for these.' He named a startling figure.

Kit clutched her throat, conscious of immense shock. 'But that's absurd!' she protested.

'Believe me, in a few years' time you won't find that very grand.'

'It's mind-boggling *now*. I can't take that much from you. No one here commands that kind of money.'

He shrugged his elegant shoulders in an almost weary gesture. 'My dear child, I've just explained to you that you're the only one for whom I'd make such an offer. Take it or leave it.'

'I'll take it!' she cried with alacrity. 'My own mother wouldn't be caught dead with one of mine, but perhaps the view is different from Olympian heights. You realise, if you change your mind, you can have your cheque back?'

'I won't change my mind.' His eyes dwelt on her chasing expressions. 'I don't understand this relationship you have with your mother.'

'Because you know nothing about it,' Kit retorted.

'I wonder.' His golden glance was very steady. 'Now, I must go.'

'Of course.' The full weight of her enthralment struck her. 'I'm holding you up—I'm sorry.'

'Don't be,' he said. 'I now own two beautiful works of art. I'll display them at the house.'

'I think you *are* trying to help me.' She followed him up.

'I am.' His half-smile was dangerous, the crescents beside his mouth deepening. 'But I know real talent when I see it. No need to feel defensive.'

'You seem to like Bohemians,' she said, for want of a better word.

'There are some tender areas in your life, aren't there?'

'What do you mean?' They had reached the front door and now Kit stood staring up at him.

'I have an instinct about such things. You haven't said a great deal to me, Christiana, but what you *have* said has given me a clear picture.'

'Of what?'

'Let's say, anxieties. A search for identity. Now, I must be off.'

The briskness of his tone spoke volumes of dismissiveness.

'Goodnight, then,' she responded, stung. 'You can't think I'm going to fling myself at your feet?'

'I don't think I could find a way of stopping you if you wanted to.'

'Oh, you beast!' She looked up at him, startled, angry, humiliated. 'When you're cruel, you're ghastly!'

Thorne looked sardonic, but not dismayed. 'I'm only being cruel to be kind.'

'Please don't bother.' Her violet eyes glittered with scorn. 'My senses are attracted to you, which you unfortunately know, but my head is very much in control—a fact you haven't reckoned with. Underneath that cool façade, you're a formidable man, and you mean to be. A woman would have to protect herself from you.'

'So?' He inclined his gleaming head mockingly. 'We're both on our guard?'

'I was that, even before you started insulting me.'

'Christy!'

Some note in his voice, some faint tenderness in his arrogant face, demolished her. It was the one thing she had not counted on.

'Stop!' Kit retreated so abruptly, she backed into the wall. 'I've never, never been called Christy, and I don't want anyone to start.'

'Why so threatened by a new form of your name?' He put out a calming hand to her, as though she were a nervous filly. 'You're so...unheralded. As beautiful and unexpected as an oasis in the desert.'

She was confounded by the strength of her feeling for him. 'I'm not listening,' she said tightly. 'You're not going to seduce me.'

'My dear, I'm not even trying. As I see it, I'm trying to calm you down.'

Even then, she knew it was true. He was withholding sexual power. What if he released it? It seemed to Kit that she had no other option but to go down fighting.

'I'll turn into a statue,' she said through clenched teeth.

'You couldn't, not with that flush of blood beating through your golden skin. I suppose you *could* learn a little of the value of passion,' he added.

'I should and I will. But not with you!'

'Why not? We do share an empathy beyond the normal.' He folded her into him with shocking suddenness, and that easy act of conquest so enraged her she began to struggle violently, unmindful of the looseness of his burgundy shirt.

'Careful, Christy,' he warned, a catch of laughter in his low-pitched voice.

'Let me go!'

'In a minute, little one. Be steady. I would never hurt you. But by the same token you must expect what you yourself have been inciting all night.'

Her struggles had an ambiguity about them. She appeared to be readying herself for the shocking touch of his mouth. But he did what she had never expected. Never, *never*. He bent her slender body back over his arm, amber eyes brilliant and mocking and full of a male power. 'Christy, Christy, you have the most beautiful breasts, like carmine-tipped roses, and you will insist on exposing them to my gaze.'

'You must be joking!' she gasped.

'You're *not* trying to stir things up?' Mockery and sensuality gleamed all about him. It flooded the air. He leaned her back even further, and even as Kit cried out protestingly he brought his mouth down on the sensitive satin skin of her upper breast.

It was astonishing: one minute she was fighting him, then her whole being was rushing towards him under some raging compulsion. If he lowered his head and drew on her aroused nipple she thought she would die of the stupendous excitement. Already there were bubbles in her brain.

'Please!' she said gaspingly.

It was the best, the worst; the most frightening, the most ravishing moment of her life. The blue veins of her breast were hot wires searing the vulnerable flesh. Nineteen years. Nineteen years. Put another way, she was being *born*!

'Don't, Thorne.' Her pleading had more than a touch of allure.

'Strangely, I can't hear you.' His voice was very deep and soft and languorous.

'You *can* hear me.' She, on the other hand, now sounded frantic. His mouth was moving closer to the tight, erect bud, the most tender and the most erotic instinct in the world.

'All right.' Abruptly Thorne lifted her, one hand shaping her head, her hair spinning out in a rose-auburn mane.

'I can't seem to stop trembling,' she admitted in amazement.

'I'm trying to get a hold on myself.'

'It's no joke!' She met his brilliant, animated eyes.

'Indeed it's not. I have strong views on cradle snatchers.'

That upset her. 'You don't appreciate that I'm a woman?'

'You look like one,' he assured her. 'You certainly feel like one, but I'm not sure.'

'Kiss me.' She straightened her shoulders and threw her head up.

One eyebrow lifted. 'Is that an order?'

'It did sound horribly like one. I suppose it is.'

'Even when you haven't the slightest experience of adult passion?'

'Don't count on it,' Kit said rashly.

'Really?' Those supremely intelligent eyes narrowed. 'Are there no bounds to young Cowley's infatuation?'

'Put it this way,' she said crisply, 'when he kisses me, he gets co-operation.'

'Christy!' He burst out laughing.

'Don't make fun of me.' She brought up her fingers to lie across his mouth.

'Which is worse?' Though he took her hand and held it, he had the look of a man determined on following his own code.

She tried to speak, mouth quivering and parted, but she was too shattered to find words. Only her eyes spoke for her, blindingly beautiful and blue without end.

'Don't do it,' warned Thorne, in a taut, clipped voice. 'You're colouring my mind.'

'I didn't start it,' she offered vaguely. The blood that beat in her ears kept rhythm with the beat of her heart. She was nearly engulfed in a delirium of arousal, cloaking her in a soft, gleaming radiance.

'You surely did,' he challenged in a hard, flat tone.

'Since when can't you handle a mere child?'

Her look of youth underscored her obvious bravado, but for once he took no account of it, moulding her to him almost savagely, tightly gathering her masses of hair and forcing her face up.

'What do you do now?' He couldn't conceal a male hostility.

'Don't ask, just kiss me,' she whispered.

There were golden sparks in his eyes and he muttered fiercely, increasing the cruel pressure and covering her soft, cushiony mouth with his own.

It was a moment of unmatchable excitement, phenomenal in its intensity. Great stabs of emotion rent Kit's breast. Her fantasies, her world of dreams, were as nothing compared to this. Her body rippled with excruciating desires, and God help her, she couldn't conceal them. When Thorne's tongue caught up hers, she jerked against him as if the muscles of his lean body were powerful magnets clamping her to him: breast, hips, shuddering pelvis, legs. The excitement was such that it

nearly stopped her heart. For all her imaginings, her un-
defined emotions, she had never thought of human
passion as utterly destructive of the will. Surely the mind
could resume control?

Maybe never. Not now!

Chaste though she was, she responded to him with a
rare sensuality, her body pressing, yielding against his.
It was exactly the sensation of melting, and finally he
had to break it.

'Where did you learn to kiss like that?' There was a
cynical curve to his etched mouth; towering male, topaz
eyes and taut features.

He had released her so suddenly, her head was whirling
with giddiness. Even his words barely registered. 'Was
that what it was?' she whispered. 'I thought I was thrown
into a furnace.'

'Either way, it was a big mistake,' he clipped. 'Put it
down to a combination of my shirt and your body beneath. You'd make a world-class pupil in the arts of love.'

'I guess you'd know, from your travels in the Orient.'
Kit blushed scarlet, but she still held his gaze. 'Do you
still want my paintings?'

'Yes.'

'There's no need to annihilate me.'

'Lock me out, then,' he shrugged.

'I will.'

It was obvious that though her spirit was strong, her
flesh was weak. Kit moved away from him in an un-
steady rush, long perfect legs, flying mane, luminous
skin, and for some reason, perhaps protective, Thorne
deftly scooped her up and carried her to the door.

'Shake yourself out a tranquilliser and go to bed,' he
ordered.

'I don't need a tranquilliser!'

He eyed her wryly. 'Then you're a first-rate actress.'

'If you mean I was staggering a bit, I'm tired,' she
explained.

'The young usually react like that in a crisis. You
wanted to be kissed, my lady, and see where it got you.'
He set her down gently, still half supporting her. 'That's

all there is to it, by the way. I'm quite a bit older and
I'm very strong-minded.'

'So am I.'

'But we're not *like*-minded. My intention, Christiana,
is to befriend you, not play out an extreme fantasy. I
appreciate that you're very beautiful and you're becoming aware of your own power, but you can't cut your
eye-teeth on me. That would be difficult and dangerous.
Your own age group is the norm.'

'You mean, you think nineteen-year-olds are
harmless?'

'More accurately, I think you could control them. And
yourself.'

Kit blinked her long lashes. 'You *do* take yourself
seriously!'

'Forgive me—but it's important that you understand
how I feel. I'm not into exploiting young girls. I'm at
war with myself even now for kissing you. And don't
confuse a little play with the real thing. Stay in love with
love for a while, Christy. Adult love does have a ruthless
side to it.'

'Is there someone *you* love? Some special woman?'
she asked.

'Not now.'

'What does that mean?' she whispered.

'I'll tell you one day. Not now. Goodnight, little one.
Lock the door after I'm gone.'

That kiss had accomplished in a few moments what
nothing else had been able to accomplish in all Kit's
young life. She felt she couldn't cope. In one bound,
she had moved beyond the security of self-control. Her
arousal was reflected in her dreams. For most of the
night she was running down an arbourway of her own
fantastic flowers, pursued by a demon of overwhelming
speed and power. Not only that, she was paralysed by
her own fascination. Thorne seemed to have golden
horns on his handsome head, and when at last he caught
her she fell back, swooning, into his arms. Her whole
body was in a state of sexual ferment. She wanted to be

possessed, devoured. It was all too, too frightening and peculiar. She didn't even get up for her early morning swim.

'What's wrong with you?' asked Melly as Kit hurried into the kitchen for some stimulating coffee.

'I didn't sleep well. How was your night?'

Melly daintily nibbled on a piece of toast. 'What can you do with your parents around?'

'Don't worry, you're beautiful enough to catch any man's attention. All you have to do is grow up a bit more and be patient. Is there any coffee?'

Melly leaned forward and picked up a beautifully decorated pottery coffee-pot. 'I notice you're not mentioning your night.'

'Give me time!' laughed Kit.

'Daddy didn't notice the van. Where did you leave it?'

At that moment, Patrick entered from the rear door that led down to the beach. 'No problem, was there, Kit?'

Both girls kissed their father simultaneously, and he added his own bear-hugs. 'Are you in the mood for a long story?' Kit asked him, with the first edge of anxiety.

'I suppose it broke down,' Melly said complacently, pouring her father a fresh grapefruit juice.

'I'm aware I have to do something about that van,' Patrick said.

Kit sat straight down in her chair, her normally straight shoulders slumped. 'The van is no more!' she announced.

'*What?*' Melly broke in, over her father.

'To make a long story short, it broke down on the way, two hippies tried to pick me up and Thorne Stratton turned up just as things were getting into a hassle. He then had to drive me home, and we noticed the van was no longer on the road. They'd rolled it out of spite, but it didn't catch fire then. It blew up as I pelted down the embankment after it. The motion dislodged it from where it was precariously braced against a tree and it burnt out in no time.'

'Good God!' There was shock and dismay in Patrick's bright blue eyes. 'It's a miracle you weren't harmed!'

'Thanks to Thorne Stratton,' Kit said, almost under her breath, and averted her eyes.

'My dear child!' Patrick gave a great, gusty sigh. 'All these years in a safe haven, and now apparently you're not safe on the roads'.'

Melly stooped over her sister with her long gleaming hair. 'That must have been terrible for you, Kit!'

'A few hairy moments,' Kit admitted.

'Wait until we tell Mummy!'

'Tell Mummy what?' Clare walked into the kitchen with her flower wrap around her.

'Kit had a terrible night!' Melly cried emotionally.

'There's always drama with Kit,' Clare smiled, and gave a faint shrug.

Patrick fixed his eyes on his wife's face. 'If you could just *listen*. I've said over and over we had to do something about that van. Kit isn't a young man, she's a beautiful young woman—someone special, unique. Women are extra vulnerable. I assume she's always safe, but she could have had a bad time last night. Two hippies tried to pick her up, and ended up rolling the van. By the grace of God, Stratton was with her and she came to no harm.'

'Thorne Stratton was with you, was he?' Clare asked almost sharply.

'Someone had to drive me home.' Kit traced a pattern over the table without looking up. 'Anyway, it's not all bad.'

'Surely, as host he wouldn't want to leave the party?'

'Obviously, he felt responsible,' Patrick said sternly. 'One would expect that of a man of his protectiveness and valour.'

'You asked him, Kit, did you?' Clare continued without apology.

'I did *not*!' Only then did Kit lift her brilliant eyes. 'Mr Stratton saw the van break down from the house. He spoke to those two creeps. It's just as Daddy said— he felt responsible. I hope you don't mind.'

'Nothing about you, Kit, is straightforward,' sighed her mother.

'Goddamn it, Clare,' Patrick cried explosively, 'they don't come any straighter than Kit!'

Clare didn't move. She only swallowed her orange juice. 'Good work, Kit,' she said.

Though she was powerfully upset, Kit hid her grief in a flippant aggression. 'It's even better,' she said. 'Thorne Stratton bought two of my paintings.'

'Because, of course, he's so nice!'

'Mummy!' Melanie intervened quickly, her loyalty to her sister becoming increasingly intense. 'I've no idea what's happening here. It's almost like a war—and are you thinking what you have to lose?'

'How could I forget?' Clare answered oddly. 'I'm sorry, Kit, what were you saying?'

'No worries.' Kit pushed an untouched bowl of fruit away. 'I'd best be off.'

'What paintings, Kit?' Patrick wanted to know.

'The parrots and my latest fantasy.'

'How could you sell *that* one, Kit?' Clare demanded. 'Quite frankly, I find it erotic, and the half-naked creature in it is obviously you.'

'I suppose the red hair was a clue!' Kit bent over and kissed her sister's cheek. 'I've invited him back to the gallery—he said he'll bring his friends. Take a tip and wear your new pink.'

'You're positively obsessed with pushing your sister forward,' Clare said. 'Melly is only a child.'

'Sure, Mummy,' Melly answered in an acid chirrup.

Patrick caught Kit up as she was surging towards the beach. 'Slow down, darling, there's a good girl.'

'What's wrong with me, Paddy?' Kit demanded.

'*Wrong* with you? God, girl, what are you talking about?'

Kit didn't answer, but ran down the slope, tears in her eyes.

'Kit, please, spare a thought for your old dad!'

Kit turned then and stared directly at her father. 'I think it's time, Paddy, that you started thinking of me. I've tried every way I know how to come to terms with my own mother's abandonment.'

'What?' Patrick's healthy colour completely failed. 'Who told you?'

'What do you mean, who told me?' Kit cried angrily, brushing the back of her hand over the long wet spikes of her eyelashes. 'If I have to say it for myself, I'm a pretty intelligent girl.'

'Why, of course you are, darling,' Patrick faltered. 'My God!'

Kit stared at him, noted his demeanour, and all of a sudden her own anger folded. 'What's the matter with you, Paddy? You've been listening to Mother for months now, so why the shock?'

Patrick shook his riotously curling head. 'Let's go back a bit now. You're talking about Clare?'

'Who else could be making me so angry?' Kit all but shouted. 'Honestly, Paddy, I think the grog is destroying some of your brain cells. I guess I was never a well-loved child, like Melly, but somehow because of you, because *you* loved me, I found a way of coping. But what's happened to Mother? I can't even call her Mother. Wouldn't that make anyone fairly anxious? I mean, it's not typical, is it? I have to call my own mother Clare. Is it possible she's jealous of my youth? Has the fact that I've grown up precipitated some crisis? Is Clare's feeling for me so complex she feels threatened by her own daughter? For God's sake, Paddy, if I wasn't such a positive person the effects could be severe. Everything about me provokes Clare's anger. She hates the way I look. She hates the way I sound. I realise Melly is the model, but surely most mothers love their children, even if they are completely different? I'm not bad looking.'

'Darling——'

'Listen, Paddy!' Kit hit her father's beseeching hand away. 'I don't want to upset you. I love you. I love Melly. I'm even trying desperately to continue to love my mother. That in itself would seem to require the forbearance of a saint, and I'm no saint. I think it's better if I just go away.'

'Let's walk down to the beach, Kit,' Patrick said heavily. 'I couldn't bear to lose you, Kit. You're closest to my heart. My love for you is no threat to Melly.'

'I know that,' she said softly.

'Of course you do. You're an exceptionally generous-hearted girl, you have been from your earliest days. The fact that you've come through so well resides in your own strength. In a way, I've failed you.'

'No, Paddy!'

'Clare has tried to be a good parent.'

Kit gave a shaky laugh. 'She's pretty grim these days!'

'As you say, it's all psychological.'

She lifted her head, and let the sea breeze caress her skin. 'Based on what, Paddy? It's only lately I've started to defend myself. Even Clare couldn't say I've been rude or difficult. I'm like you, I'm very easy-going. At the same time, unlike you, I'm not all for the quiet life. You must have noticed that Melly is becoming affected. I don't want to divide this family, but I can't continue to be treated with this weird hostility. *Clare doesn't like me.*'

Patrick turned her toward him and took her gently by the shoulders. 'Have you ever thought Clare knows you have the greatest claim on my heart?'

'But, Paddy, she's my *mother*!' Kit very nearly sobbed.

'She can't talk about it, darling.'

'None of you can talk about it,' Kit pushed back violently, her violet eyes brilliant in her golden-skinned face. 'What are you asking me to do? Sometimes I think if I pulled out of here you'd all fall flat on your face. You're a clever man, but you've opted for a life I just don't understand.'

'It's a long story, Kit,' her father sighed.

'Oh, Paddy, *Paddy*!' Kit threw her arms around her father and hugged him fiercely. 'Can't you talk to me?'

'What is there to say, darling? Clare has never had the knack of showing you just how much she cares.'

Kit lifted her glowing head. 'She has no difficulty with you, with Melly. In this last year or so, *I* seem to have become the personification of the kind of woman Clare

least cares about. I suppose it comes to all children
sooner or later, whether their parents really approve of
them or not. When I was younger I tended to take the
view that there was something wrong with *me*; now I
think there's something wrong with Clare. I thank God
for my nature, Paddy. It's helped me keep my balance.'

'Let me talk to Clare,' Patrick pleaded. 'The way I
see it, it has a bit to do with the menopause.'

'What men won't blame on the menopause!' said Kit
ruefully.

For the first time, Patrick grinned. 'You know your
mother is going through a difficult time.'

'I *am* trying to handle her with kid gloves.'

'How else can we account for it?' Patrick said breezily.

'Well, you haven't come up with anything sensible so
far. Clare is only forty-four.'

'Nevertheless, a difficult period. I dread these little
occasions.'

'Sure you do, Paddy, but the hurt is more particularly
mine.' Kit stared down at the sparkling blue water.
'Thorne Stratton thinks I have real ability. If I went to,
say, Sydney, I could get a job and study at night.'

'Out of the question!'

'You can't keep me here for ever, Paddy,' Kit breathed
quietly.

'I'm aware of that, darling, but I want you to stay on
a while—at least until you're twenty-one.'

'Oh, Paddy!'

'What is this Stratton like?' Paddy asked suddenly.

'Powerful!' Kit looked up at her father with a feeling
glance. 'He's a very serious person.'

'Why wouldn't he be?' Patrick shrugged. 'I guess he
wanted to know why you were driving around in that
rattle-trap?'

'Do you think I have real talent, Paddy?' Kit asked
abruptly.

'I do, but then, I'm your father.'

'No, no, Paddy, I'm a big girl now. You must begin
to level with me.'

Patrick remained immobile, his gaze fixed on the sapphire shimmering bay and the islets beyond. 'You paint, even now, with a beauty and assurance I could never attain. And I'm good, Kit.'

'You don't know *how* good!' she told him.

'Oh, I know, darling. But some things are more important than making a name.'

'Why, Paddy? What are you afraid of?'

'Why do I feel so lousy?' Patrick shrugged.

'I guess, because I'm upsetting you. What are you staring at?' It seemed to Kit that her father's regard was, for once, highly emotionally charged.

'I'm staring at you.' Patrick lifted his hand and traced the pure line of his daughter's cheek. 'You're so beautiful and so strong. I used to think nothing else would matter, but, oh, you matter to me.'

'Paddy, forgive me.' Kit sounded weary and unhappy. 'What are you talking about?'

Patrick lost the steady, concentrated look in his eyes. 'How much did this Stratton offer you for your paintings?'

'Enough to buy a second-hand van.'

'My darling girl, I simply can't allow you to spend any more of your own money. *I* propose to replace that old bomb.'

'I was hoping you'd say that!' Kit laughed.

Patrick nodded and put his arm around her shoulder. 'We must stay together, Kit. It's what I've lived for. What I'll die for.'

CHAPTER FIVE

THE INCIDENT of the van caused a commotion in the small, closely knit community, even after the vandals had been neatly spotted and apprehended by a cruising constable.

'I can't believe it. I simply *can't* believe it!' ex-Brigadier Campbell told Kit in his epiglottal bark. 'Damn fortunate Stratton was with you. First-rate chap, that! Thought he'd come up here for a nice little holiday and look what he got. Wretched scoundrels! What they need is a stint in the Army.'

Kit managed to escape before the Brigadier moved into full throttle. Most of the young men of the district had been told they were a slack lot.

The rest of the community was just as grateful. Within a remarkably short time, Thorne Stratton had become the local lion. Kit wondered if he were on the point of packing up and going.

'Awfully handsome, isn't he?' female after female said in a file. 'So glamorous. Such an exciting career. Imagine you meeting him like that!' Even Kit was pinching herself.

Patrick was the first to invite him to dinner, even if he had to wait until Thorne Stratton had waved the last of his guests off, including the scare-making Alyce Schaffer.

Finally it was the night, and Melly was looking spectacularly beautiful. The day had been spent in almost total inertia, but as soon as the sun set her zest for self-perfection was limitless.

'How do I look?' she asked Kit for the ninety-ninth time.

'Ravishing!' Kit assured her briskly. 'Do you think you can move away from that mirror?'

'Of course.' Sweetly, Melly moved to Kit's bed.

'I don't like to leave too many things undone.' Kit considered her own appearance in the mirror. 'There's nothing worse than having to dive in and out of the kitchen.'

'Just don't forget it was Mummy who did it all,' Melly warned.

'Just for once, I'd like to take the credit.'

'You really like him, don't you?' Melly urged with soft gravity.

'Certainly I do,' Kit responded flippantly. 'He's gorgeous.'

'I wonder how old he is?' mused Melly.

'I would say, thirty-three or four.'

'And that voice!' Melly watched Kit apply her make-up. 'I didn't know anyone could speak so beautifully.'

'My dear, providing one is upper class English and has gone to the right schools...'

Melly gave her delicious giggle. 'I wondered if Mummy would take to him, but he's so charming.'

'Which is more than one could say for his girlfriend.'

'Do you think she *is* his girlfriend?' Melly pursed her pink lips. 'I thought she looked like a snooty clothes-horse, and she wasn't a bit nice. Not too many people leave the gallery without buying something. Everyone else did. I imagine she thought she was slumming.'

'Yes, indeed, a common lot.' Kit dismissed the thought of Alyce Schaffer. 'I hope Paddy keeps off politics.'

'What's got in to Mummy lately? She's certainly picking on you.'

'Must be the time of the month.' Kit ran a trace of blusher under her cheekbones. 'Don't worry about it, pet. I suppose we all see one another from a different perspective. You're the sort of daughter Mother wanted. I used to hold to the theory that mothers just naturally loved all their children, but it's simply not the case. I imagine you look just like Mother did at the same age. My looks, personality, are too dominant. Essentially I'm a woman of a different family—perhaps Paddy's great-

aunt. You know, the one who became a missionary in
West Africa.'

'I think you're wonderful, Kit,' Melly said softly. 'You
are, and always will be, the best sister I could want.'

'I know what you mean,' Kit smiled. 'I love you too,
precious girl. Now, which dress do you like on me?'

Thorne Stratton arrived at the very moment he was
expected, bearing wine and chocolates. Melly was openly
transfixed by him, so much so that it became a problem.
Kit, on the other hand, was very brisk. Not that he wasn't
a sight to make a strong woman go weak at the knees:
the cream of essentially British good looks with a touch
of the torrid. His clothes were classic, elegant: beautifully cut tan trousers, a soft cream collarless shirt, a very
classy rust-coloured jacket. His dark golden hair was
brushed back, and his taut, chiselled features wore a relaxed, charming smile.

All of them had met him before from his brief visit
to the gallery; now Patrick welcomed him with outstretched hand. Even Clare, in her favourite shade of
blue, looked soft and flushed and happy. It struck the
sensitive Kit powerfully that she herself was the only fly
in Clare's ointment. Most of the time with Melly and
Patrick, angers, resentments, jealousies, whatever, simply
didn't arise. It was very difficult to understand, but plain
to see.

Clare was even saying now, 'We couldn't allow you
to leave us, Mr Stratton, without thanking you properly
for saving Kit from the results of her own rashness. We
can't pretend she's not reckless to a fault.'

Thorne Stratton's cool, handsome face didn't change,
but Patrick rushed in with words to the effect that most
people would be very upset when they saw their car
rolled.

In some ways, it was an evening of great contrasts.
Pleasure, a rising excitement in such a stimulating guest,
Patrick's predictable provoking arguments, which their
guest not only enjoyed but neatly confounded, and the
continuing secrecy about the family background. In

short, Thorne Stratton, correspondent extraordinaire, was discreetly but insidiously probing their background. Their present state he knew, and it was becoming increasingly difficult for Patrick to dodge the direction of a social interrogation. At least, the highly aware Kit saw it that way. Even Patrick couldn't duel with a past master at ferreting out information. Most people would have been more than happy to supply the story of their lives, but *her* mother and father banded together to keep the past at arm's length.

It was release, of a fashion, to escape to the kitchen. She had planned the meal thoroughly, with their own oysters Rockefeller, followed by a casserole dish she had perfected in the last month: firm white fish fillets and prawns in a subtle white-wine-flavoured sauce, served on a bed of spinach and garnished with piped cream potatoes around the edge of the dish. It was gratifying to see their guest eat with relish and for Clare to blush with pleasure when she was complimented on the meal. Kit was content. She would have moved heaven and earth to please her mother. It had to be, she often thought, the central emotion of a child. All young longed for love and acceptance, and what was one without the other? So preoccupied was she with serving the meal, she scarcely noticed what she ate, but she did intend to relax with coffee and a marble cheesecake she had lavishly decorated with long chocolate curls. She had even toasted and finely chopped hazelnuts to improve the flavour.

'Do sit down, Christiana,' Thorne exhorted her, rising quickly to take the heavily laden silver tray.

'I'm going to,' she smiled. 'I thought—Mother thought—we'd have it out on the deck. I love sitting above the tree-tops.'

'Great idea!'

Patrick was keen to tell Thorne how he had built the house: the local timbers that had been used, the tables and chairs he had made. Thorne appeared so interested it had the effect of going to Patrick's head. Never had they had such stimulating yet such sympathetic company.

'Show Thorne'—he was *Thorne* now—'the portrait you did of Kit and me,' Melly suggested, the soft light falling directly into her dazzled eyes.

'I'd very much like to see it.' Thorne turned to her and smiled. 'Your father is blessed to have three such lovely womenfolk.'

'Of course, I'm like Mummy,' Melly pointed out proudly. 'Kit thinks she must look like our great-aunt, the missionary.'

Patrick poured more coffee and passed it to his wife. 'What aunt would *that* be?'

'Just a joke, Paddy,' Kit smiled.

'It would intrigue anybody,' Thorne Stratton murmured smoothly. 'Kit doesn't really resemble anybody.'

'What, you don't think she looks like me?' Patrick demanded jovially.

Thorne shook his gleaming dark blond head. 'I dare say it would be easy to find a likeness in your photograph albums.'

'If we had any,' laughed Melly. 'We might as well be orphans.'

Clare leaned forward and touched Thorne on the arm. 'The portrait is hanging in our bedroom, if you'd care to see it,' she told him.

'Indeed I would. Kit told me how very good it is.'

'Judge for yourself,' Patrick suggested wryly. 'I wouldn't think of pushing myself.'

The master bedroom was decorated in the subdued pastel shades Clare liked, the furnishings sleek and spare so that the large portrait that hung above the bed appeared to capture all interest in the room. Patrick had had it specially lit, as one has to do to make a painting most effective, and now the girls' faces and light, graceful bodies were bathed in vibrant light. Melanie, in delicate pink, was seated in a beautiful Louis-Seize bergère Patrick had actually borrowed from Brigadier Campbell, and Kit in a rich yet misty shade of blue was gently poised on its arm, her limbs lighter, longer, more elegant, her red hair falling in masses of curls and waves. Both girls

looked directly at the artist, and their separate personalities could not have been more dramatically presented.

'My flame and my flower,' Patrick said gently. 'My
two beautiful daughters in all their grace and beauty.'

The tears sprang to Kit's eyes at the depth of tenderness in his voice, but their guest gave Patrick a concentrated glance. 'Now I know the source of Kit's gift.
This is superb!'

'It is, yes,' Patrick agreed absently. 'Beauty has to be
illumined from within. The spirit must shine through
the flesh. I always had it in my mind. I simply waited
for the girls to mature sufficiently to capture their essential natures.'

'Wonderful!' Thorne stared at the radiant canvas.
'With such ability, you could be making a considerable
name for yourself. This is a true portrait—the insight
into character! Perfect features count for little without
spirit and intelligence.'

'Mummy thinks it would have been better balanced
had Kit looked more composed,' Melly told him. 'As
you can see, she's nearly springing out of the canvas.'

'How right you are,' Thorne agreed crisply. 'What a
perfect name for each, my flame and my flower.'

'I feel happier being a flower,' Melly said. Patrick
laughed and drew her to him, kissing the top of her head.

It was one of the best nights they had ever had, and
with exquisite timing their guest decided to depart at the
very height of their pleasure.

'Wonderful evening!' Patrick declared enthusiasti-
cally as they all filed along the silver canyons of the
garden. 'How strange that Kit should be the one to
prompt you to write of your experiences.'

'I suppose she wants to do the typing,' Melly piped
up artlessly. 'I know you'll write a very powerful novel,
Thorne. You're so witty, yet you're so serious!'

'The seriousness of the world's problems has been
brought home to me, Melanie,' he told her gently.

Kit trailed behind. In reality, she was a little tired. If
one wanted a dinner party to be so successful one had
to work hard. Above them, the stars were as prolific as

wild flowers, every star in the universe packed like diamonds on black velvet: white, rose, yellow, Vega, Capella, Betelgeuse. Their most famous constellation, the Southern Cross, had once been visible in ancient Babylon, but the Crux had drifted over the many centuries into the southern skies. The star nearest the South Pole was a star of the first magnitude, and tonight it appeared extraordinarily brilliant. So intent was she at looking up that Kit stumbled over a protruding moss rock and thudded gently against Thorne Stratton's wide, lean back.

Somehow he had learned enough of her body to catch her unerringly around her narrow waist, pivoting towards her so that for a moment they looked like lovers carried away by the fragrant night and the scent of gardenias.

'Really, Kit, can't you watch where you're going?' Clare scolded lightly. She turned to their guest and spoke to him. 'Frankly, I'm not sure what to do about Kit. She's so headlong about everything!'

'The stars are beautiful enough to absorb anyone's attention,' he deflected her comment smoothly. 'I must thank you, Clare, for a delightful evening. Dinner was superb.'

'Yes, we're very proud of Kit's cooking,' Patrick exclaimed thoughtlessly, putting his wife in an embarrassing position.

'You mean, Kit did all that?' Thorne asked drily.

'No, sir, I helped. Clare lets me have a bash at Christmas,' Kit put in hurriedly.

'Why, Patrick, *why*?' Clare asked afterwards. 'You made such a fool of me!'

'You certainly did,' Melly seconded.

'I'm sorry, my darling. I celebrated too much at dinner.' Patrick was determined to hold on to his good humour. 'Anyway, Kit saved the day.'

'You think so? You really think so?' Clare's clear voice resonated strangely.

Melly's big eyes widened. 'She did say she *helped*. Why don't you say you hate to cook, Mummy? Nobody cares. We really appreciate all the other things you do.'

It was a mammoth struggle for Kit not to snort. She, in turn, was smarting over some of Clare's remarks.

Clare turned and stared at her. 'I know what you're thinking, Kit.'

'Don't make things more difficult than they already are. I thought the evening went very well,' Kit parried.

'He probably knows you're infatuated with him,' Clare said witheringly.

'Who said anything about infatuation? God!' Patrick burst out wrathfully.

'How can you be blind to it?' Clare looked at her husband with a hint of contempt.

'Mummy,' Melly said quietly, 'Please!'

'I'm worried about Kit, that's all. She's so ungovernable in all she does, and it could be her undoing.'

'You don't care how much you hurt me, do you, Mother?' Kit accused, unable to keep the smarting tears from her eyes. 'I can't turn to you for anything. I must be *made* to feel an outsider. Tell me seriously, did you really have me at all?'

These words so ignited Patrick that he actually wrenched at his wife's arm. 'I'm telling you, Clare, your attitude is not only upsetting the girls, it's upsetting me. I accept that you're concerned about Kit's zest for life, when everyone else is impressed by it. *I* think Kit is very mature for her age. Why don't you just take it easy and let her pace herself? Picking on her every ten minutes will have her bolting through the front door. And I'm telling you, Clare, *I don't want that*!' He looked towards her, for once acting formidable.

'Let's forget this whole thing!' Melly begged.

'I apologise, Kit, if I've been hurting you.' Clare turned away quickly, looking fatigued. 'I didn't mean to, but my anxieties for you are heartfelt. It worries me enormously who you will be.'

'*Who*, Mother?' Agitated, Kit jumped to her feet. '*Who* I will be? Isn't that an extraordinary thing to say?

Would anyone blame me for thinking there was a lunatic in the family? Is that it? There's insanity in the old family tree?'

'Kit, please!' Patrick went to his daughter and took her firmly by the shoulders. 'You're talking nonsense. Perhaps we're all living too closely.'

'I'll move out.'

'Will you allow me to finish?' he said urgently. 'Instead of building that coffee shop you've always wanted in the garden, what about if I build you a little garden house of your own? You're growing up, and you want to be your own woman. You're the most domesticated of young creatures, but you have a decided mind of your own. The little hassles you and your mother are having are a complex issue. Sometimes, parents can't accept that their child is grown up. A garden house will provide you with a place of your own, but you'll still live in the family environment. That's what I want.'

'Better still, I'll move in with you, Kit,' Melly declared with uncharacteristic force. 'That's a great line you're handing us, Paddy, but to my mind it's like kicking Kit out, and I won't stand for it!'

''Ray, 'ray, 'ray!' said Kit, both smiling and sad. 'I don't know what I'd do if Melly didn't love me.'

'You think *I* don't?' Patrick said quietly, his blue eyes glazed. 'I'd give up anything for you, Kit.'

'We haven't been seeing much of the world,' Clare tossed in in a tight, dry voice. 'What your father is saying is true. He has considered you first all your life. *You* have always been his prime consideration. Melly and I just get what's left.'

The bitterness in Clare's voice sobered Kit abruptly. She had never really considered that her own mother could be jealous of her, but the closest human relationships sometimes took exaggerated forms. Clare was such a reserved woman—instead of being able to talk things out, she had allowed her disturbed feelings to go to ground. The tender-hearted Kit immediately felt remorseful. She was always looking for a reason for Clare's unreal attitude, and this was it.

'I never realised you had such painful feelings, Mother,' she said, her eyes fixed beseechingly on Clare's face. 'You know in your heart that what you're saying is not true. We're hurting each other, and for no good reason. It's not a thing either of us intends, it just happens. I'm not going to make a fool of myself over Thorne Stratton. Gorgeous as he is, I'm perfectly well aware that he's way out of my league. But I can look, can't I? Even Melly's eyes were glazed over. Perhaps Paddy is right—we both need our own space. It would cause a lot of talk if I shifted to the other side of the Cove, but a garden house sounds ideal. The only thing that worries me is, where is the money coming from?'

'Where, indeed?' Far from looking soothed, Clare raised her delicate brows.

'You let me worry about that,' Patrick said firmly. 'Now, I think we should all go to bed. In my experience, a few drinks loosen the tongue, and people say lots of things they don't really mean. Speaking of breaking down...' he began to walk about turning off lights, '...there's an almost frightening power in Stratton. He makes you feel you have to, not even want to, tell him the story of your life.'

'Then may I make a suggestion?' Clare slammed the sliding door shut. 'Avoid him. Avoid him like the plague.'

Thorne himself made that easy. Kit didn't see him for another ten days, and then only briefly, when he dropped off an order. In the intervening time, she had tried to convince herself that her tumultuous feelings were only accelerated hormonal development; the trouble was, she was tuned into the powerful mind behind the handsome skull.

'You've been writing, haven't you?' she demanded.

'I have,' he confessed.

'And that's it? You're not going to tell me about what?'

He looked down at her, eyes like gemstones in the now deeply bronzed cast of his face. 'Would you believe, a love story?'

'I don't think a book is wholly satisfying if it doesn't have human passion at the centre,' Kit told him.

'And you're an authority on passion?'

'I've had my explosive moments.'

'If they were just over a week ago, forget them.'

'Have *you*?'

'You're a very forward girl, Christy.'

'I really get browned off when men say that. I would have thought you were more liberal than most.'

'I am usually,' he smiled at her. 'With other women. I've never had a personal relationship with a teenager.'

'Who turns twenty on the fifteenth.'

'Really?' The mocking expression softened a little.

'Please, if you're thinking of a present make it dinner at Port Perry. They have a dream of a restaurant.'

'Hugo's On the Beach?'

'The very one. Not everyone can afford Hugo's prices—but then, not everyone can afford a Jaguar.' She let her eyes wander from his brilliant eyes to the smile brackets beside his mouth. She wished he didn't have them; they made her heart thud alarmingly.

'What about the family?' asked Thorne. 'Aren't you celebrating at home?'

She pushed her silky sleeves up her arms. 'The family settled for a present—as a matter of fact, a big one this time. Paddy is building me my own private retreat.'

'Just like that! Why?' His eyes searched her face.

'Because I'm a big girl now,' she said with deliberate faked sweetness.

'Or because you're getting in Clare's hair?'

'How dare you!' she said darkly. 'You don't know anything about it.'

'I know your mother gives you a hard time.' The topaz eyes became hooded and unreadable.

'Is it that obvious?' she asked with a defeated sigh. 'You certainly know how to play a trump card.'

'What is it you do, Christy?'

'I don't do anything. Believe me,' she protested with forced humour.

'And where is this private haven to be?'

She raked back the riot of curls that were moving forward on her face. 'In the garden, of course.'

'One would hope not out of calling distance?'

'You actually sound angry!' She looked up at him in surprise.

'Aren't you?'

'No.' She shook her head vigorously. 'What do I care if my mother doesn't like me? Paddy does, and Melly's so angry she's gone on a diet. It's no crisis. There are good and poor relationships in lots of families. Don't they always say two adult women can't exist in the same house?'

'So...this...alienation is fairly recent?'

'Mind your own business, Thorne Stratton!' Kit said crossly.

'Not while there's breath left in my body. You need help, Christy. You can't continue the way you're going. This store!' he glanced around him impatiently. 'It won't do. You should be continuing your education in a stimulating, demanding society. You have a great deal to offer. Your artistic gifts for one so young are impressive. There are other things to be, Christy. *Better* things.'

'All right, all right.' She began to dart about the store as if she were some mouse in a cat-and-mouse chase. 'What do you want me to do? I have no money.'

'I said I believed in you, your talent. Why should I not back you?'

'Well...' she said uncertainly, 'you might want to make me your mistress when I'm twenty-one.'

'I've got other fish to fry, and don't you forget it. I ought to slap you for that.'

'I don't care if you do. Anything you do is impossibly erotic.'

'No matter. *You're* safe. I have a strange feeling about you, Christy, call it my sixth sense. Why does Patrick always change the subject when one asks about your early life?'

'I hate to say this, but I think there's a mystery in the family,' Kit confessed.

'You don't remember anything as a child?'

'I remember falling off a swing and Patrick bawling his eyes out. There's nothing bad buried in my subconscious. We were a peaceful family. Mother always favoured Melly because, I guess, she's so like her. By the same token, Paddy had a special bond with me. Certain personalities need certain things. I was never a clinging child, I always wanted to do things for myself. Maybe I didn't allow my mother to play a big enough role—I don't know. In any case, I've given up wondering now.'

'You're very generous,' Thorne said. 'Plenty of other girls would have bitterly resented their baby sister, but I can see you never have.'

'Resent Melly?' Her violet eyes flashed. 'Melly is the best thing in my life. I was always the protective one, but these days she rushes to my defence. I'm the catalyst that disturbs the harmony of life.'

'What a damnable situation!' he sighed.

'I must be crazy, telling you so much. You have the sort of eyes that burn into one's soul.'

He didn't smile back, but continued to stare down at her with vertical lines between his winged brows. 'I take it Patrick's at home? I'd like to call round.'

'What for?' Kit felt faint with anxiety. 'You're not going to start something?'

'Why else would I go?' he said almost harshly. 'No, really, Christiana, I like your father, even if I'm none too sure why he acts as he does.'

'Start asking questions and the friendship might founder.'

'Why, if there's nothing to hide?'

'There's nothing to hide. Don't be ridiculous!' she flared. 'What do you want to know for, anyway?'

'Because whatever it is is slowly destroying you. The Judge told me he *had* seen you before,' Thorne added.

'The man at the party?'

'Yes.'

'I'd never seen him before in my life!'

'How can that be, when he knows you? Or your face. For reasons *I* don't understand, you were quite familiar to *me*.'

'We met in a past life,' said Kit flippantly.

'And we weren't strangers there, either.'

She laughed, a wild little sound. 'I think perhaps you'd better go. You unsettle me enormously.'

'I guess that goes for me, too.' He leaned forward and gave her a painful little tap on the chin. 'Montville out of bounds without young Cowley?'

'Sure, until I get the van.' What was happening to her voice? It sounded soft and husky.

'I imagine he's hoping to take you out for your birthday?'

'I don't know anything about that.' She dipped her head.

'Word is, he's adored you since you sat in the same classroom.'

'You know it was a one-room school? Glenn is two years older than I am.'

'And I understand his mother depends greatly on him?'

'For a man who's just moved here, you know an awful lot,' said Kit ruefully.

He nodded. 'Mrs Russell is a mine of information. If you can bear to commit yourself into my care, I'd be delighted to take you out to dinner for your birthday.'

'And Alyce? How's Mrs Schaffer?'

'I wouldn't expect a little cat not to have claws.'

'No, really—I wouldn't think of telling you my story if you won't tell me yours.'

'Funny you should mention Alyce,' he remarked. 'She wants to come again, and bring a friend.'

'Missed you, eh?'

'Whatever in the world are you driving at?' he asked blandly. 'Alyce is only a friend.'

'Can I quote you?'

'Indeed so.' He stared her down.

A shadow approached the doorway of the store, quickly followed by its owner's ample figure. Signora

Campigli, a lady well known for keeping an eye on things. She paused, with a ludicrous attempt at discretion, obviously sensing the tension, her liquid black eyes, so full of intelligence, darting with roguish interest from the flushed girl to the imperturbable male figure.

'Always I hope to see you, Signor Stratton,' she announced in the fruity voice that suggested she fancied him greatly, 'and you are here!'

Kit bent her head quickly, concentrating on the shopping list so as not to burst out laughing, but Thorne Stratton turned to the new arrival like a veritable prince.

'Buon giorno, signora, comè sta?'

It was the start of a four-minute conversation conducted entirely in Italian—was the man a polyglot?—in which the Signora dropped thirty years right in front of Kit's eyes. The fervour with which women worshipped the male of the species! No more splendid a creature walked or moved or talked upon earth than Man. The good Lord knew the value of women, even if they didn't know it themselves. It seemed very much as if Woman could never hope for a higher status than Man in this earthly life. Her position could even be confusing in heaven. What was all the more caustic was that Man accepted this idolatry as his right. Her whole sex was beset by automatic male worship. Mothers, for example, were very keen on their sons—look at Glenn. Many of her girl friends didn't get quite the same commitment as their brothers.

'Why, Christiana, are you looking so serious?' the Signora paused briefly to demand. Her cheeks were flushed and her eyes were extravagantly bright.

Why, indeed! 'I'm pondering a very profound question: the inequality of the sexes,' Kit informed them with mild sorrow. 'Men are born the masters.'

'Impossible!' the Signora spluttered into rich laughter. 'It is women who make men their slaves! Isn't that so, Signor Stratton?'

'Based on my experience, *signora*, yes.'

'When I would have sworn you weren't a man to give in without a struggle,' Kit returned promptly.

The Signora, looking at them, considered matters had progressed.

CHAPTER SIX

IT WAS Melly who suggested they ought to have a party for Kit's twentieth birthday.

'How many people are you thinking of, Kit?' Clare stood on the upper balcony, looking out at the sparkling and serene bay.

'I wasn't thinking of anything,' Kit protested mildly, alerted to her mother's tone. 'It's Melly's idea.'

'And a good one,' Melly returned simply. 'I love parties. Besides, a twentieth birthday is a special occasion.'

'I always thought that was reserved for twenty-one.'

'Really, Clare, I don't want a party,' Kit said good-humouredly. 'I'm all right the way I am. Parties cost money, and I'm still the cook around here. I know just how much work a party takes.'

'But I want a party,' pouted Melly. 'I want to dress up and have fun. I want Gl—*men* to notice me.'

'Men?' Kit asked in a startled voice. 'I thought you were going to say *Glenn*.' Something came to her in a flash. Melly had always liked Glenn.

'Don't be silly!' Melly flushed. 'Everyone knows Glenn worships the ground you tread upon.'

'Maybe,' Clare inserted drily, 'but that would never work out. Glenn's not tough enough for Kit.'

The normally placid Melly faced her mother with intensity. 'Isn't that the wrong word to use about Glenn? I would have thought he had lots of toughness and tenacity. Look how hard he works.'

'You don't understand, darling,' Clare said soothingly. 'I meant tough as in dash and fire. Glenn is too tame for Kit.'

'I don't understand what all this is about,' Kit said as mildly as she could. 'Glenn is my friend.'

'You're not a friend to *him*, my girl!'

'No, you're not, Kit,' Melly leaned towards her sister. 'He loves you—I've told you that.'

'How can he love me when he doesn't *tell me*?' insisted Kit.

Clare picked up the cup of coffee she had set down seconds ago. 'Probably because he's seen you and his mother together.'

'And what does *that* mean?' Kit's quick temper rose.

'Don't get on your high horse with me, young lady,' Clare warned. 'There's something about you none of us can quite name. You're not an easy person to handle. Glenn would be quite out of his depth. His mother knows this.'

'She's spoken to you, right?' Kit's violet eyes flashed.

'Not in so many words.' Clare glanced away. 'It's easy to see she's worried about your...friendship. She was worried when you were still in high school.'

'I thought Kit was rescuing Glenn from his mother?' Melly burst out loyally. 'She's absolutely fear-ridden about losing him.'

'All the more reason he should choose a girl his mother wants.'

'That's ghastly,' Melly shuddered. 'Victorian. Everyone feels sorry for Mrs Cowley, but she can't run Glenn's life. He can't keep up with his friends. She's frozen nearly all of them out except Kit. No wonder he's close to Kit! She's a real pal!'

'Thanks, Melly.' Kit felt a quick rush of gratitude. 'I suppose I am a little concerned about Glenn's changing feelings. I wouldn't hurt him for the world, but I could never think of him as anything else but a friend.'

'Really?' Melly spoke so hastily, she had to check herself. 'Do you mean that, Kit?'

'Why, of course I do, baby. Surely you're not carrying a torch for Glenn?'

'Don't be ridiculous, Kit!' Clare said shortly. 'You think I'd allow Melly to waste her life on a small-time farmer?'

'You must know the farm is quite profitable.'

'You're never happier, Kit, than when you're trying to take a rise out of someone,' Clare maintained. 'I have plans for my daughter.'

'You're saying you have only one daughter?' Kit shrugged, cool on the outside, heart pounding oddly beneath.

The tender-hearted Melly looked as though she was on the verge of crying. 'I thought we were talking about a party, right? That's what *I* was talking about.'

'Look, I have to go,' said Kit, 'Don't worry about a party for me, Melly.'

'You have a real chip on your shoulder, haven't you, Kit?' Clare said mildly. 'Of course you can have a party, if you want to. You can do anything that suits you. Goodness knows, we have enough room.'

'That's why Paddy has ordered timber for a garden house.'

'You would say that, of course.' Clare took another swallow of her coffee.

'Why don't you two act as you used to?' Melly asked unsteadily, and waved her hands in front of her.

'That's not easy any more.' Kit shook her auburn head. 'I'm not sure we were ever really close.'

Melly looked shocked. She looked at her mother, then she turned back to Kit.

For a moment, no one spoke, then Kit offered finally, a throwaway thing, 'In any case, Thorne Stratton has asked me out to dinner—Hugo's On The Beach.'

Clare didn't move, but Melly jumped up from her wicker chair in excitement. 'I'm dumbfounded, girl! You mean that gorgeous man in *his* position has asked little ol' you to dinner?'

'Well, you know——' Kit assumed an idiotic pose.

'You lucky, lucky thing!' Melly declared with enthusiasm.

'You know it won't do,' Clare's sharp tone dispersed the frivolity. 'He's much too old for you, much too worldly and experienced. I can understand his interest in you, but I resent it at the same time. You have parents who care about what you're doing.'

'When it suits them,' Melly put in gamely. 'Who was around when the van blew up?'

'And what *is* his interest in me, Mother?' Kit met Clare's grey stare steadily.

'You know that as well as I do.' Clare tightened her loose cotton shirt over her. 'I would have thought he was a gentleman in the true sense. Now I see he's not.'

'Because he asked Kit out to dinner?' Melly asked incredulously. *'Mother...'*

But Clare warmed to the subject. 'A sophisticated and highly literate man could have little in common with Kit, except one thing,' she insisted.

'I trust you're not going to mention *sex*!' Kit tilted her abundantly curling head.

'Don't be impertinent with me!' For the first time, there were angry lights in Clare's grey irises. 'Some women attract men like flies—women like you, Kit. There's something audacious in your expression, something highly inflammable. For God's sake,' she snapped her fingers, 'you don't think I *want* to point these things out?'

'Why not? You've been doing it for ages. Did someone like me try to take Paddy off you, Mother? Is that it?'

'How *dare* you!' Clare cried, much too loudly.

'Why are you so thin-skinned about yourself and so insensitive about me?' demanded Kit, pale-faced. 'You speak about me as if I were some incipient Jezebel, some wanton creature without mind or morals. I find it offensive. I'm almost twenty, yet no one yet has managed to seduce me—and don't think they haven't tried.'

'Hear, hear!' Melly cried. 'Some of them are really lecherous.'

'And how would *you* know?' demanded Clare.

'Oh, *Mum*! That's all boys ever think about.'

'It's clear,' Clare said finally, 'that you're a bad influence on your sister.'

'Rubbish!' Melly grasped her mother's arm. 'It's you, Mummy, who won't let me grow up. You're always speaking about things for "your own good". Kit's good, and so am I. You're overly protective.'

'And there's nothing wrong in that.' Clare began to stack the coffee-cups together. 'Certain things are not suitable. In a month or so, Thorne Stratton will go back to his glamorous life. Probably, he'll never set foot up here again. What earthly use is it for Kit to break her heart over him? No one could possibly ignore the fact that he's an extremely attractive man. And underneath that oh, so smooth exterior he's a man of strong passions. That's the dangerous part. Besides, he's involved with someone else.'

'Not that appallingly smug blonde?' snorted Melly.

'The woman he brought here, Alyce Schaffer. It was easy to see they're something more than friends. And why not? They're mature people, and unattached. I would much rather you have your party, Kit, than contemplate any candlelit dinner with Thorne Stratton. I know your father would agree.'

'So let's ask him,' Melly said.

'He's too old for you, darling,' Patrick murmured, looking down through the crystal-clear water. The wind had fallen away, and they were becalmed on the boat, far out in the bay. 'Too much a man of the world, too experienced. What are you, after all, but a green girl?'

'I thought that's what men liked best of all, green girls?' said Kit.

'So they do. I'm not arguing with you. Most men's interest in women is sexual, then all the differences crop up.'

'He's only asking me out to dinner,' Kit pointed out mildly.

'Only you're head over heels in love with him.'

'*Paddy!*' Kit's vivid, passionate face flushed.

'Well, aren't you?' Paddy rolled over, resting his chin on his hands.

'I don't know what I think about the man,' Kit evaded. 'All I know is that since I've met him he's torn my safe little world apart. Sometimes I think he's as dangerous as the devil himself.'

'Why? What has he said to you? *Done* to you?' Paddy demanded.

'Don't be an idiot, Paddy! Nothing. He's a gentleman in the old tradition.'

'Oh, sure!'

'He *is*, Paddy.' Kit swept back her salt-crisped hair. 'You can't deny that you like and admire him.'

'Which is not to say I wouldn't fill him full of holes if he harmed my daughter.'

'He's not the sort of man to derive satisfaction from hurting women. His whole image is one of strength and seriousness. I would say he was a man with a high moral tone.'

'And I'd agree.' Paddy turned his head to look into his daughter's eyes. 'The thing is, my darling, I'm quite persuaded he's attracted to you, though you're whole worlds apart. I think he's decided not to recognise it, because of your age and inexperience, but you've found a chink in his protective armour. I'd be surprised if you didn't. You nearly stop *my* heart.'

'Love you, Paddy,' Kit leaned sideways and rubbed her head against her father's sun-tanned shoulder. 'I think he does find me attractive. To some extent I've been working on it. It's a marvellous feeling to know oneself a woman. To be a woman is the most beautiful thing of all. I don't see myself as a sex object. I don't overvalue my looks—such as they are—but I think it's glorious to be able to incite desire. I expect it's immature, playing the temptress, but I'm having a lot of fun.'

'Because you're counting on his intelligence and integrity. It wouldn't be quite such fun if he were thinking of a spot of rape.'

'Don't be ridiculous,' Kit laughed. 'You know the man and so do I. Much more to the point is *my* behaviour. Maybe I'm a bold hussy, just like Clare says.'

'She doesn't mean it, Kit,' Paddy protested.

'You bet she does!' Kit gave a wry laugh. 'Do you want to know something else I think odd?'

'Odd?' Paddy's bushy blond eyebrows rose, and his expression changed to one of uncertainty.

'Clare doesn't want me to see anything of Thorne. Not because she's worried I might get hurt with some impossible dream—that's the basis for *your* anxiety. Clare's objections aren't as simple and basic as that. I've come to feel she's actively—dare I say it—*jealous* of me. The more so as I've grown up. Maybe I'm too female or something. Maybe she resents *our* closeness. Maybe she resents anybody being attracted to me. I have a need to make sense of this, Paddy, and I can't. All I know is what I feel. Clare's attitude towards me is neither maternal nor caring—it's far removed from her attitude towards Melly, none of us can deny that. You didn't have a big affair at one time?'

'I'm going in for a swim,' muttered Paddy.

'No——' Kit grabbed his hand hard. 'You stay here. Don't feel too guilty, Paddy. Just *tell* me.'

'What on earth gave you that idea?' Paddy demanded almost angrily. 'I've been a completely faithful husband.'

'So, all right, simmer down.' Kit's brilliant deep blue eyes were fixed on her father's face. 'Hang on—you said husband. What about before you married Mother? Were you madly in love with a woman who looked like me?'

'For God's sake, Kit!'

'Why are you so afraid, Paddy?' she persisted.

'My dear girl, you're talking absolute nonsense!'

'You're slipping away, Paddy. Your eyes aren't meeting mine. I'm still holding your arm, but you're withdrawing, aren't you? I'm only trying to get to the truth.'

'No matter what?'

'What the heck, Paddy!' Kit sat up as if shot. 'Is it true?'

'Honey, honey!' Paddy buried his curly head between his arms.

'You did have an affair, Paddy. Is that it? Now I see...she had red hair?'

'I did know a redhead,' mumbled Paddy. 'What's wrong with that?'

'Why all this secrecy?' Kit wondered. 'You once had a redheaded girlfriend. You split up, then you married Mother.' Kit laughed a little wildly. 'Poor old Mum was jealous. She's been jealous all her life.'

'There *was* one special person, yes, Kit.' Paddy lifted his head, his deep voice faintly hoarse, as though the words cost an effort. 'Maybe it explains a little of Clare's irrational resentment.'

'It explains a lot!' Kit searched behind the genial blond façade her father presented to the world. 'You old dog, Paddy!'

'An ordinary story, isn't it?'

'What was her name?' she asked.

'I've forgotten.' Paddy traced the flight of a sea-gull.

'What a lie, Paddy,' Kit sighed just under her breath. 'Do you suppose Clare has seen me as a rival? Do you think her unhappiness has stemmed from that? You just said yourself, human beings aren't rational. Somehow, because of the colour of my hair, she has always connected me with the other woman. It's downright unreasonable, but I do so want to understand.'

'If I were you, darling, I'd leave well alone.' Paddy rearranged a length of rope. 'Clare is too touchy about a lot of things.'

'My God, could she hold on to a thing like that?' Kit protested. 'Could she punish her own child for having memorable hair? That's fantastic!'

'So it is,' agreed Paddy. '*You* made it up.'

Kit shook her glowing head. 'You're the ultimate evader, Dad. This is a disturbing story. I always knew there *was* one.'

'I must ask you not to mention it to your mother.'

'Wouldn't talking it out help?'

'No, Kit, it would *not!*' Paddy burst out almost violently. 'Lots of mothers and daughters keep their distance. It happens with fathers and sons. There's no way we can make relationships perfect; they just develop. In a sense, you're none of Clare. It's simply a matter of your taking solely after my family. Melly is familiar to her mother. You're not. You're so different, it's complicated things enormously. At each stage you're like a young tree throwing out more branches, more blossoms. Maybe we all retain a primitive streak. Maybe at her deepest, most secret level, Clare *is* jealous. It's her cross.'

'Had you tried, Paddy, it mightn't have had to be mine,' Kit said quietly.

'Ah, darling,' Paddy said bleakly, 'don't blame me. I picked myself up and plunked myself down here—all for you. So you could grow in peace.'

Kit's dazzling eyes widened significantly. 'What's the matter with the cities? You make it sound as if they're all prisons!'

'Let's say my motivation was peace and security.'

'In anyone else, Paddy, that would be paranoia, and I don't associate paranoia with you. It's *Clare* who has the serious hang-ups.'

'It's a good thing for both of us that compassion is a central part of your nature. Now, there's a wind springing up,' Paddy announced with obvious relief. 'I'm thinking old Oskar might be coming by. Thorne was telling me he's going to try to establish contact. Apparently he had the glasses on you and Oskar the other day, and found it fascinating. I told him you're the only one Oskar will allow to touch him, though he's friends enough with me to take a fish from my hand.'

'Why not? Dolphins are people. The reason Oskar allows me to swim with him is because we began contact when I was a small child. For some reason, that made us equal. It's odd, though—he'll swim away if Melly comes into the water.'

'It's incredible, really,' Paddy agreed. 'Thorne wants to film it.'

'Perhaps Oskar will let him. I don't really want a party, Paddy. Why don't we just drop it?'

'I don't want to see you become involved with Thorne Stratton, sweetheart,' Paddy declared. 'If you were several years older, I would never stand in your way. But he'll move on—you know that. From what little we know of him, it's obvious he was bred into high circles. We can all see his magic. He's something of a legend. He's used to drama, glamour, excitement.'

'What we're all after, I expect. There are many things *I* want to do, Paddy. I've got capacities I haven't even begun to tap.'

'Give yourself time, sweetheart,' Paddy implored. 'You're only twenty. I feel panic-stricken at the thought of losing you before you're ready to go. If I'm going to be entirely honest, I'd say I'm panic-stricken that a man like Thorne Stratton has found his way up here. Underneath that suave, controlled exterior, you've kindled a spark. You're both aware of it, but you must know he's decided you're little more than a child. You've only started on the voyage of self-discovery. He's a much experienced man—that's it in a nutshell. It's all too easy for him to have you madly in love with him. It's alarming. Unhappy love affairs are torture. The pain, the implications, can remain for a lifetime.'

'It sounds as if you know, Paddy.' Kit was on her feet in one graceful movement.

'So I can't be cool about it,' Paddy confessed. 'Enjoy Stratton's company if you must, but be sensible about it. Believe me, my darling, he's a man to be reckoned with.'

Kit tried to make a joke, but it wouldn't come off. She was desperate for the thrill of danger, even if it brought her a broken heart. Her feeling for Thorne Stratton was as inexorable as the pull of the tide, as elemental. Nothing could change that, not now or ever. He had gathered all her life in, in one moment.

The wind whipped at the sail.

'We ought to be getting back,' said Paddy. 'Plan whatever pleases you for your birthday. Fill the house with your friends. Invite Stratton. I have to admit, he's the most stimulating, the most confident and charming man I've ever known, but he's only here on a visit. The whole world is his oyster. Speaking of oysters...' Deftly, from long practice, Patrick changed the subject.

Oskar was waiting for them a short distance from the shore, and Kit stripped off her T-shirt and shorts and

dived overboard. She gloried in her unique friendship
with this beautiful creature from the deep, and as the
dolphin drew alongside she reached out her hand and
rubbed it around the snout.

'Welcome, lovely boy. I've missed you!'

The dolphin returned her beaming smile, its bright eyes
filled with a warm and friendly light. Water streamed
from the bulging melon on its head, and its whole
expression was one of innocent pleasure. For a wild sea
creature it was entirely unafraid and as faithful and delightful a companion as the most outstanding domestic
pet. Just like the star performers in aquariums, Kit had
trained it to fetch a rubber ball, and at different times,
when he was in the mood, Oskar leapt high into the air
to take a fish when offered from the prow of the boat.

Now the dolphin rocked gently on the sapphire,
glistening water, waiting for Kit to initiate some game.
He wasn't as large as other dolphins she had seen—
something under eight feet, but his powerful fluke and
flippers made him a swift, graceful swimmer, excelling
in sudden turns and stops, deep dives and amazing leaps.

Treading water, Kit ran her hand affectionately along
the mammal's solid dark grey sides and silvery under-
belly—something Oskar enjoyed as much as any dog
loves a rub—but she always kept her hand from the
opening like a nostril at the top of his skull, the blowhole.
It just happened that her earliest instincts had been right.
Dolphins did not permit rubbing on the top of their
heads. The blowhole led down to the air passages used
for breathing, so the blowhole had to be kept clear. It
always seemed incredible to her that dolphins could
drown.

'How would you like your picture taken?' Kit asked
the smiling creature. 'You could be famous!' She and
Oskar were already famous around the bay. There was
no danger in living in such a protected environment,
where everyone looked on their special dolphin as some
enchanting gift from the gods. Only there were sad stories
about wonderful dolphins who had befriended man;
now, more than ever, the world was full of cranks. No

one was ever going to harm her beautiful Oskar. Thorne could take his film if he liked, but it would have to be for private viewing. She had never forgotten how she had cried when a New Zealand friend of Paddy's had told her all about Pelorus Jack, the marvellous dolphin who had brought the ships through Cook Strait for more than twenty years before being shot by some sick human being.

The afternoon sun turned the fine spray to gold. The wind was freshening, rippling the turquoise sea. Kit arched her back and went into a dive, the signal for their game to commence. Oskar was even smart enough to occasionally allow her to beat him to the rocks, where she sat with her knees drawn under her, applauding his answering performance. It was a kind of miracle, after all, for girl and dolphin to meet in perfect harmony.

Everything was decided over dinner. They would ask around sixty people to the party, combining Kit's circle of young friends with older family friends and many of the artists' community who regularly showed at the gallery.

'Business and pleasure!' Patrick commented with satisfaction, and reached for the wine bottle. 'It should be a great night, Kit. And just so you don't tire yourself out with all the preparations, let's hire Mrs Russell to do a lot of the catering.'

'That's if Thorne doesn't mind,' Kit stipulated.

'Aren't you going to ask him?' Melly implored.

'He mightn't want to come.'

'He'll come.' Clare looked up from her meal with a dry-as-bones expression. 'Sexual attraction is a very powerful force.'

'Excuse me, Clare, but I've discussed all this with Kit,' Patrick said. 'Common sense will prevail.'

'It never did for you.'

'You've changed, Clare,' Patrick said simply, and got up from the table.

'I'm sorry.' Clare glared almost accusingly at Kit. 'Please sit down again, Patrick. I can't help it if I'm disturbed by Thorne Stratton's unexpected entry into our lives. The change in Kit is too rapid, and I associate it with the man. Someone has to introduce a note of caution.'

'Is it worth saying that Thorne would be astounded at your anxieties?' Kit's blue eyes blazed up to meet Clare's. 'All *I've* said is, he's quite gorgeous. Out of liking, he invited me to dinner. God knows what your mind is running on!'

'You don't fool me, my dear,' Clare said sweetly. 'You're as dangerous to Thorne Stratton as he is to you. I just don't want to be left with the consequences. I've had enough to deal with in my life.'

'I never knew you were so puritanical!' Kit pushed back her chair. 'I doubt if he would want to come, anyway. It might even be best if we don't have a party.'

'Certainly, it would save money,' Clare answered quite sharply. 'Why can't you be gracious, Kit?'

'Oh, I'm sorry. Perhaps you could show me how.'

Angry colour rose in Clare's cheeks.

'I don't want anyone to say any more,' Patrick said in a quiet, threatening voice. 'It's incredible the change that's come over this family.'

'Please, don't think of starting on the garden house, Paddy,' Kit begged emotionally. 'I've thought it all over, and it wouldn't work. The Griersons are letting their bungalow while they go overseas, and I know they'd trust me to take it on. Afterwards, when I'm free of my commitment at the store, I'll move on. After Thorne has seen my work, I'm hopeful I'll be able to do something with it. I'm hungry for new experiences, independence. I couldn't bear to make an enemy of my own mother.'

No one had taken any notice of Melly, who was clenching her fists in frustration. 'Why does everything have to end the same way?' she shouted. 'Can't we all be happy and affectionate? What's got into you, Mummy? Kit works twice as hard as anybody, and what does she get for herself? Perhaps she should go somewhere else. You're picking on her all the time. But I'll tell you this: *she* goes and *I* go!'

Clare sprang to her feet, reaching one arm out towards her younger daughter. 'You don't understand, darling—at your age, there are so many things you don't understand!'

Melly's breath came faster, but she laughed. 'I understand, Mummy, that you're leading a kind of double life. You're so indulgent and caring with me, yet you act as if Kit isn't worth it. If *I* wanted a party, you'd sweep every consideration away. Anything *I* want, I get. Kit wants a party, and you don't like the idea very much. Can you blame her for feeling the way she does?'

'Please, Melly,' Kit turned away to the picture window, 'don't say any more. We've shared some good years. Don't take it all away.'

'Mummy, *say* something!' Melly implored.

'I'm sorry, Kit,' Clare answered on a defeated sigh. 'Truly sorry. I can't seem to help what's happening to me. Don't think I'm not aware of it. I know what a good girl you are. I'm very grateful for your valuable support, but we seem to meet head-on.'

'I'm sorry too, Mother,' Kit said quietly. 'I must be putting an intolerable strain on you. I have a better insight now, a better understanding. Perhaps we both need a breathing space, so that when we come together we'll see our best qualities. I think I'd enjoy being on my own for a while, so perhaps the Griersons' going away is a godsend. You can visit me any time you like, and I can visit you. We're not far apart. Melly must remain here, of course. *I'm* the one who's threatening your contentment.'

'God Almighty!' Patrick exploded violently.

'*Please*, Paddy! Can't you see it's all for the best?' Kit asked spiritedly. Unconsciously, she had pulled back her shoulders and tilted her head, looking very much a young woman of character and purpose.

'I don't believe this!' Melly said in a choked voice.

'No.' Patrick's bluff, handsome face looked tired and drawn.

A silence fell on all of them, Melly's rounded young body turned towards her mother, as though waiting for her to speak. But Clare remained hunched up in her chair, as unapproachable as ever; she was in her worst mood.

'It's all settled, then.' Kit contemplated her family, her emotions under tight control. 'I'm leaving because I love you, not out of any sense of rejection. I suppose things like this happen when parents suddenly find themselves faced with adults instead of children. I would never want you to feel guilty, Clare, because we're not dealing with one another particularly well. Life is as it is, not as we might wish it to be. Personally, I think we'll get on much better if we don't see quite as much of one another.'

'Close living does make difficulties, Kit.' There was something haunted and forlorn about Clare's expression. 'Please forgive me for my shortcomings. I *try*.'

'Try, hell!' Melly jumped up abruptly and ran from the room.

'I'll go after her,' said Kit.

'Please,' Clare answered in a muffled voice, 'I couldn't bear to lose Melanie.'

That, more than anything, set Kit on her course. The same afternoon, she visited the Griersons and found them first full of wrath; then after, Judy, the wife, had settled down, full of understanding. Although Kit told a story of an urge for independence, the Griersons, as long-time friends, were well able to read between the lines. Many people, it seemed, had become aware of emotional conflicts within the Laccy household, and Clare, with her high level of reserve, had not exactly endeared herself to her neighbours. In the end, the Griersons refused point blank to take any rent at all from Kit. All she was required to do was look after the bungalow and garden.

'We're delighted we'll have someone we can trust,' Judy Grierson assured her. 'I can see it's been a difficult decision for you, Kit, but sometimes we all need a little impetus to start a new life. You're such a clever girl, too. You want to find more time for your painting.'

Patrick took it badly, though he bought Kit a brand new Suzuki carry-van to help ease his conscience. Kit called it her 'birthday present'. All talk of a party had been dropped, and Melly, who had always seemed such a child, grew up overnight.

Glenn was one of the first to notice. 'Do you ever notice Melly doesn't chatter any more?' he asked Kit almost absently, as he visited her at the Griersons' house one afternoon.

'That's pretty normal. She's all grown up.' Kit was noting the surprised expression on Glenn's face. He, more than anyone, had always treated Melly as a baby.

'She's going to be beautiful, too,' he realised.

'What do you mean *going* to be? Melly has always been beautiful.'

'Yes, but in a little dolly sort of way. Even Mum has noticed the difference in her. Your breaking free has woken Melly up. She's more involved and caring. Overnight, she's lost all her babyish habits.'

'You mean, overnight, she's left behind adolescence. It happens. I did too much for Melly,' said Kit. 'She realises that now. She flunked out of high school because she was so lazy. Now she's looking at herself with new eyes. I think Melly is going to surprise you. She's my sister and I think she's special.'

'Even Mum said she brightened up the place,' Glenn offered. 'The three of us had a cup of tea the other day after we dropped off your things. Melly poured out her soul to Mum, and Mum could see she was so upset she really tried to help. You know how uninterested Mum can act, but Melly compelled her to listen. The two of them were going at it hammer and tongs. Mum said she had a vague idea of Melly that simply wasn't true. I was surprised. The two of them got on really well—not like *you*. Mum sort of feels safe with Melly, which is a pretty odd thing to say, but somehow it's true. I'm not suggesting Mum doesn't think the world of you, Kit, but you're so bright and sort of positive that Mum might feel she's a kind of failure. Melly turned her around.

Perhaps the clearest way I can put it is that Mum obviously needs people to need her.'

'And I don't come into the "safe category"?' Kit tried to keep the hurt out of her voice.

'You're strong, Kit,' Glenn said simply. 'You're the sort of girl others lean on. When Dad was alive he used to call you a real little heroine, and you were only a kid. Maybe being brave is drawn out of extremes. Melly has always been pampered and coddled. Your mother has had a lot of difficulty admitting she loves you. She sure didn't pamper you in any way. Even Paddy has always given you the freedom of a boy. A lot of us were anxious about you in that old bomb, and even then it took a stranger to prevent you from coming to harm. Sometimes I wish Thorne Stratton had never come here,' he added. 'He's almost caused a revolution.'

'You mean he expresses opinions that make people think?'

'He's certainly popular with you.' Glenn made no attempt to hide his jealousy. 'Who does he think he is, anyway? Some sort of authority figure? He's even checked this place out.'

'Just because he called?'

'He might have been expecting a terrorist attack,' Glenn persisted. 'He walked all around the grounds—I'm sure he checked the doors and windows. All in that fearfully cool way of his. I think he's battling an attraction to you.'

'Nonsense!' Kit broke off a spray of jasmine and waved it under her nose.

'Then I find it most odd the way he looks after you. I think you ought to consider that he's more aggressive where you're concerned than Paddy is. He's also seeking Paddy out, I suspect to chat him up.'

'About what?' Kit's eyes flashed.

'How should I know?' Glenn gestured vaguely. 'He has no right to make Paddy suffer. Paddy's suffering enough. He hates you here, but he doesn't want to break up his home. You're sure not a typical family. If I didn't know better, I'd swear Clare wasn't your mother. Mum thinks she doesn't know *who* she is.'

'I'm not the child she wanted,' shrugged Kit. 'Anyway, let's forget that. When and where did you see Paddy and Thorne talking?'

'Last night, if you want to know,' Glenn told her doggedly. 'They were down at the marina. Paddy looked for all the world as if he'd been stopped by a top detective. He had that same funny look on his face, as if he feared he'd been found out.'

Kit pulled the pins out of her hair and it came tumbling down. 'That sounds so theatrical!' she said flatly.

'It looked that way, too. Could Stratton possibly have anything on Paddy?'

'My God, Glenn!' Kit laughed shakily. 'What could Paddy have possibly done wrong? I can't help knowing Thorne doesn't approve of my being here on my own, but he wouldn't insult Paddy by taking him to task. Paddy is my father. Thorne is——'

'Go on, say it,' Glenn urged intensely.

'A friend.'

'He acts as if there's no one else to help you. *I'm* here.'

'And I'm very grateful.' Kit thrust her hands into the large pockets of her flower-splashed skirt. 'Don't be jealous of Thorne, Glenn. It's so ridiculous.'

'I suppose it is,' Glenn admitted grudgingly. 'Not that I don't admire him like hell, it's just that he so identifies with you. He knows you so well, you'd swear he'd known you all your life. He sees things in you even I don't know about. I told him I loved you, of course.'

'*What?*' Kit sprang to her feet, and walked to the ornamental timber balustrade that surrounded the sun porch.

'When you're with him, you crave to tell him everything,' Glenn confessed. 'I guess that's what makes him a media hero. He'd make a masterly interrogator as well. A man like that could get you to admit to anything. He seems to possess powers. Have you ever looked into his eyes?' A ludicrous note of panic entered his voice.

'I haven't been that close to him,' Kit lied.

'Absurd. Absurd, girl. Handsome as he is, it's his eyes you notice, first, last, the works. They send out some kind of magnetic wave. He's so damned intelligent, I swear he comes from another planet. Could that be it, do you suppose?'

'I don't think about it,' Kit lied again, when her feeling for Thorne was like a life sentence.

'Everyone tells lies.' Glenn moved quickly and seized her wrist, turning her to face him. 'Even you, Kit. Didn't he tell you his girlfriend is arriving this weekend?'

'He did.' Kit met Glenn's sparkling eyes coolly. 'She's a real sweetheart, too.'

He bent her slender arms and pulled her into his chest. 'Where shall we go for your birthday?'

Now Alyce Schaffer was arriving Thorne might look on his kind offer as a sacrifice. 'Yes, where?' Kit echoed, trying to hide her sick disappointment.

'Why not the best seafood restaurant in the entire State?'

'Can we afford it? Melly will want to come.'

'Not Melly—you and me. You and Melly can go out to lunch.'

'I can really only eat one full meal a day,' Kit prevaricated.

'*Please*, Kit,' begged Glenn. 'Dare I kiss you, do you suppose?'

'Why not? On the cheek. I'm very fond of you.'

'I prefer your mouth—it's so soft and full and luscious.'

A kind of inertia came over Kit. So often lately she had invoked the touch of Thorne's mouth. Had he only kissed her in her dreams? Some sexual fantasy that had come to her in the small hours?

As he sensed her lack of resistance, Glenn's strong young arms tightened insistently. He was mad for her—*mad*. Yet always he had been obedient to her signals. Now her beautiful eyes were veiled, half shut, her mouth was parted and a pulse beat in her long throat... '*Kit!*' he breathed, his arms trembling at her submission. 'My own beautiful girl!'

His kiss was so gentle, so reverent, it brought tears to Kit's eyes. Did she really need to hurt her friend? Her best friend, outside Melly.

'Glenn, *please*!' She loved him. She *did* love him, but not in the way that he wanted.

But Glenn was lost, reverent one moment, ardent the next. He had his pride. Kit dared not deny him, for fear of wounding his young manhood. Out of need for another, she had invited Glenn's embrace, and it was too sweet not to be easily tolerated. Her mind was free to make comparisons. No bells rang, no tremendous sexual turbulence broke around her. Thorne had raised her to another dimension. Thorne . . . *Thorne*.

In his excited state Glenn's hand moved caressingly to her breast and Kit sobered abruptly. *'Glenn!'* she protested.

'Darling, please!' Glenn was flushed and near delirious. Kit was wearing a low-necked, front-buttoned fuchsia blouse, and his fingers slipped the top button and began to close over the golden, satiny slope.

Kit shook her head back violently, her auburn mane tumbling down her back so that the man who suddenly rounded the rear veranda of the house was confronted by a seemingly most passionate scene. He stopped short, possibly surprised, but not embarrassed. He was too urbane for that. What did it matter who was kissing Kit so hotly, while she writhed in arousal? He might even have turned back to where he left his car, only newly laid gravel crunched beneath his advancing feet.

Glenn straightened abruptly with a look of dazed disbelief, but Kit, in that first moment, scorned fixing her blouse.

'I don't know how to apologise,' Thorne offered suavely. 'I knocked at the front, but you seemed to have vanished into thin air.'

'I'll bet you won't risk it again,' Kit said shortly, then instantly regretted it. 'How are you, Thorne?'

'Excellent,' he said. 'I'm glad you've got Glenn for company.'

'Hi, Thorne,' Glenn said quickly, colour still staining his clear skin. 'Listen, I'd better run. I have to find Tim Blakely, he's organising some temporary help.'

'I'll see you out,' offered Kit, making to follow him.

'No, it's all right, Kit.' It was obvious Glenn was in a state of mild agitation. 'I'll give you a ring tomorrow. It might be as well if *you* ring Hugo's—I could get too busy to get to the phone.'

'Sure, I can manage it,' Kit smiled.

''Bye, Thorne.'

Thorne waved.

'What's new?' asked Kit, taking her time to turn. Her hair was getting too long; it cascaded to the middle of her back.

'Let's start with you.' His brilliant amber eyes passed over her—hair, eyes, skin, the deep oval of her blouse, short skirt, slender gilded legs in narrow, open sandals. Glenn hadn't left her with a skerrick of lipstick, but her naturally rosy lips scarcely needed the extra gloss.

'We didn't hear you,' she shrugged.

Thorne gave her a half-smile and nodded. 'I'm happy to ignore the whole thing.'

'On the contrary, you're just waiting for the moment to tell me I'm making a big mistake.'

'Ah!' he jeered.

'I hate it when you act so superior,' sighed Kit.

'I wouldn't be so unkind as to say you're used to inferior people.'

'You can't be referring to Glenn?'

He moved back, leaning against the balustrade and watching her closely. 'Glenn's a decent young man, anyone can see that, but he's only human. You're making a big mistake, allowing his passion for you to flame up.'

'Is passion a sin?' She was trembling slightly, unfolding before his eyes. It was something he had taught her.

'The danger is that the moment would come when you would want to flee from it and Glenn wouldn't. One doesn't need superior intelligence to see you're not the least in love with him. Something deep has evolved, but your feeling for Glenn is of a different nature from his feeling for you. He believes himself to be irrevocably in love with you, and that's going to take a lot of shifting. The two of you, to an extent, live in a closed world. If you allow Glenn to kiss you, the way he *was* kissing you, you can't expect him not to get carried away. The problem is compounded now that you're living alone.'

'No problem!' Kit declared emphatically. 'I dare say you sleep with women when you feel the need. Sex is supposed to be an enriching experience.'

'Don't take your young friend for a lover, Christiana,' Thorne warned her. 'I don't think he could take it when you ran away.'

'You've lost your mind!'

'Have I?' There was a kind of contempt in his tone. 'Real desire would be the only justification, and you were only pretending, weren't you?'

His words stung. 'Why don't you ask Glenn?' she challenged him.

'I don't think so, but I do know what he feels for you. Allow him to cross the line and he'll have a lot of trouble crossing back.'

'You don't hesitate to speak your mind, do you?' She moved away abruptly, because she had an irresistible urge to touch him.

'It's a compliment of sorts, Christy. I start to get angry when I think of you living here alone.'

'Indeed?' She swung about, tilting her chin. 'Is that what you were talking to Paddy about?'

'When was this?' The sunshine turned the sweep of his hair to dark gilt.

'At the marina.'

'I take it someone saw us?'

'I have a lot of friends,' shrugged Kit.

'Patrick is far from happy about your being here,' Thorne went on. 'Even in this sheltered place, young girls—*beautiful* young girls—can be a target. Given male aggressions, no one is ever going to be able to change that. I realise you have many friends keeping an eye on you, but the nagging anxiety is the same as if you were wandering the streets.'

'We're talking about Paddy?'

'I think I'm talking about myself. You're such an appealing little witch, you've got under my skin.'

'Come and I'll make you a cup of coffee,' Kit interrupted.

'Don't smile at me, Christy.' His mouth twisted slightly.

'Why not? There's great security in knowing you're a man of the world and not easily distracted. Sit down and watch me,' she said, when they entered the delightful small kitchen. 'What a wonderful weekend you have in front of you! I understand the warm and lovely Alyce Schaffer is due to arrive?'

'Let's say, short of being very rude, I couldn't put her off. Or the Senator.'

'Gosh, is *he* coming?' asked Kit, brushing back her auburn hair. 'What a stimulating world you live in!'

'I have a feeling you'll be entering it very soon.'

There was an odd note in Thorne's voice, a fleeting expression that crossed his face, that disturbed her. 'So why do you say that?' she asked.

'Don't you want to? You're no simple little soul, Christy. You've been constantly pushing upwards from the day you were born. It's in the blood.'

'Really? Ambition isn't a feature of my family. Paddy could have accomplished a great deal and he never did. My mother is an inward-turning woman. Melly's one aim is to be a happy wife and mother. I think she'll always live largely through her husband and children. I'm a much more complicated person altogether.'

'That's a consequence of being extremely talented. I want you to meet the Senator.'

'I don't think so.' Her vivid face took on a closed look. 'I don't know if you were serious or not, saying you were going to take me out to dinner for my birthday but, as your friends will be here anyway, I'm going with Glenn.'

'I thought as much,' he said bluntly. 'However, I want you to come to the house, and I won't take no for an answer.'

'Pity—I'm going with Glenn,' she told him airily.

'You think you can refuse me when you promised me that evening? I think not, Christy. Bring Glenn, by all means. I've already asked Melly. She's a little pet.'

'And can't you remember what happened at the last affair?'

'That was a big mistake. I think you'll find Alyce will keep her distance.'

Kit poured coffee into the two cups and set the jug down. 'You want me there. Why?'

'I've put myself out a lot for you.' Idly, he stirred in a teaspoon of sugar. 'You should be pleased.'

'A part of me is pleased, part of me isn't. No, thank you, and thank you all the same.'

'You wouldn't do this to Melly, surely? She's dying to come.'

'I suppose so.' Kit frowned and bit her lip. 'I'll have to speak to Glenn. I'm rather short on a decent dress.'

'Believe me, a length of sacking would do,' he assured her.

Sensuality slipped through the banter, piercing Kit's soft flesh. 'I guess I can take care of that,' she said a little shakily. 'I haven't *promised* anything, Thorne.'

'Oh, but you have!'

CHAPTER SEVEN

THE THREE of them arrived together; Melly in a romantic rose silk taffeta she and Kit had picked out together and which suited Melly's soft, enchanting looks to perfection; Glenn in his one and only tan suit, lifted quite out of the ordinary by the Giorgio Armani shirt Kit insisted he buy and which his mother had described as 'heinously expensive and quite the wrong colour'; Kit in an outfit she had made herself out of a glorious length of turquoise silk jacquard: a long-sleeved wrap top, widely sashed, over classic evening trousers. With her long slender legs, straight shoulders, narrow waist and slender hips, it was a look that worked brilliantly for her.

Melly had been moved to wear her long fair hair in a very pretty, updated evening chignon, but Kit had settled for lots of lift and volume, an extreme to her narrow all-over look. The result, given a professional approach to her make-up and grooming, was truly stunning.

'Oh, wow!' Glenn cried in some amazement. 'Whose eyeballs are you going to knock out tonight?'

Kit declined to answer and kissed his cheek. She could scarcely admit that impressing Thorne was the key factor in all her efforts. The positive approach she carried to all her undertakings had reached new highs. 'Raw country bumpkins' they might be, or so Alyce had described the locals, but Kit considered with relief that they looked as good as anyone when she swept a good, clear critical eye around the party. No one could deny that Melly was fantastically pretty, Glenn looked positively dashing and she had made a great job of her trousers and top, even if she had been really pushed to finish it. The colour was absolutely glorious.

Unlike Glenn, Thorne just accepted her new-found glamour, although he told Melly she was the living symbol of spring.

'Would you mind doing the same for *my* morale?' Kit challenged him, and the look he gave her made her feel all of a sudden weak at the knees.

'I'm not about to turn your head, but I promise I *do* have a present for your birthday,' he told her.

'Really?' Her blue-violet eyes sparkled.

'If you don't mind waiting?'

I'd wait about a thousand years, thought Kit.

'Now, let me introduce you to everyone,' Thorne said, and as Glenn and the girls turned around Kit caught Alyce Schaffer's narrowed, hostile glance. She was standing at the far side of the huge living-room in a small conversation group, and whatever she murmured to the man beside her he looked towards Kit immediately, his mouth falling ludicrously half-open.

It was the beginning of a highly charged night.

'Isn't it silly, but I think that woman hates you,' Melly whispered as they came together about an hour later. 'Every time Thorne breathes a word to you she looks daggers!'

'Never mind, I'm having a wonderful time. What about you?'

'Exhilarating!' Melly enthused. 'Someone told me I looked like a Pre-Raphaelite angel. That woman over there looks somehow familiar—the one with the beautiful snow-white hair and the cheekbones. I haven't seen pearls like that, either, except on the Queen. She's been looking at *you* a lot.'

'You mean Lady Eliot?' Kit turned discreetly and threw a quick glance towards a private niche, where a beautifully groomed elderly lady exuding prestige and power was holding a select court. Senator Gower, silver-haired and smooth-tongued, was anchored to the love-seat beside her, while Lady Eliot was in laughing conversation with Thorne, who was bent attentively over her, holding her hand. 'She seems familiar to me, too.'

Now that it was mentioned, Kit dredged it up from her subconscious.

'It may be because we've seen her in the papers or something.'

'It couldn't be anything else. She gave me such a strange look when we met. If she weren't so singularly self-assured I would have thought she was collapsing inside.'

'So, who's the creep who won't leave you alone?' Melly whispered, then waved excitedly to Glenn across the room.

'Some friend of Frau Schaffer's,' Kit told her. 'He's divorced, and has one child living with his ex-wife. He's an architect and, if he's to be believed, enormously successful, and he's invited himself to see my paintings. In fact, he's paying me so much attention, I feel downright uncomfortable.'

'He's not the only one,' Melly pointed out simply. 'Even Glenn can't get used to your new look. You've got such enormous style! Why, I bet if you only had the wealth you could go and sit beside that imposing old lady. Instant family. You and she have that certain something that makes you stand out.'

Glenn came towards them both, eagerness in his face. 'Someone over here wants to know all about Oskar. They're not sure I'm telling the truth about you, Kit. Come and tell them yourself.' He put out an arm to Melly, who suddenly clung to him. 'Just think, I have two beautiful girls! No one guessed you were sisters. After all, you're not a bit alike.'

'Only we *are* sisters, and we'll love one another for ever and ever,' Kit exclaimed between amusement and an odd presentiment she was at a loss to account for. 'I just hope no one gets the fool idea of chasing Oskar around the bay. He's protected. He comes and goes at will.'

'Talk to Thorne about it,' Melly suggested. 'That's if you can prise him away from you-know-who.'

Whatever room she was in, whatever she said or did, Kit felt herself the centre of a circle of curious and measuring eyes. She would have thought she was there primarily because Thorne had befriended her, yet that didn't explain the intensity of response. Surely the Senator didn't have to look at her so searchingly? He was a man who dealt daily with success, beauty and power. Likewise, Lady Eliot. Something wasn't quite right. For reasons quite beyond her, she was the real focus of attention, and it wasn't because of the eye-catching outfit she had on. It could be that Thorne had excited interest in her by showing her paintings, but her highly intuitive antennae recognised that it wasn't that, either.

The architect, Bart Madden, continued to stalk her, a flagrant dissipation in his deep-set dark eyes. He was a handsome, cultivated man in his mid-thirties, but Kit wasn't pleased or flattered by his interest. In fact, she didn't like him. As he lightly grasped her arm and attempted to steer her out on to the enormous deck of the second level, Thorne suddenly materialised like the perfect, watchful host.

'Ah, there you are, Christy. I need you inside. You don't mind, do you, Bart?'

'But you're breaking up something beautiful!' Bart complained.

'I wouldn't tell that to Alyce,' Thorne commented lightly.

'Just whose girlfriend is she?' muttered Kit as Thorne propelled her away.

'You must know she's not mine.' He looked down at her suavely. 'Actually, she didn't even tell me she was bringing Bart.'

'When all else fails, there's jealousy.'

'Do I *look* jealous?' he shrugged.

'You're a very cool customer. Very cool indeed.'

He bore her off along a private section of the house that included the pleasant, relaxed room the Senator used for a study. The furniture was mainly modern, augmented by a few antiques: a massive mahogany desk and a side table lined with dozens of photographs of well-known faces. A lovely smiling photograph of the Queen occupied pride of place, flanked by a serious Prince Charles and a sensitive portrait of the Prime Minister.

'Our Senator knows a lot of important people,' Kit commented. 'All he needs is President Reagan.'

'I'm sure he's working on it,' Thorne agreed drily.

'Now, what *is* all this?' She swung to face him, looking impossibly young and daring, yet full of a female power.

The little brackets beside his mouth swiftly deepened. 'You've just got to take the initiative, haven't you?'

'Tell me. Tell me now!'

'So impetuous, Christy! Rushing into something the consequences of which you can't possibly foresee.'

'Let's take one thing at a time.' She quickly lowered her revealing eyes. 'I'm talking about my present.'

'Of course. What more could you want beyond that?'

'Well—— ' She gave a little gurgling laugh. 'I wouldn't mind a kiss to go with it.'

'It's going to be hard to say no. Wouldn't you agree?' His amber eyes were working their dangerous alchemy.

'Don't worry, I've turned into a very well-behaved, cool and poised woman,' Kit assured him.

'Fine. I was talking about me. I am aware of your technique.'

'Technique? I haven't got a technique.'

'What do you call the way you look tonight? That outfit, for example, packs the punch of dynamite.'

'Thank you. With any luck, it might cause you to collapse.'

'I'm strong, Christy. *Very* strong.' Yet Thorne let his eyes show his appreciation of her.

'Why do we always talk about this?' She stared up at him with her blue-flame eyes.

'I didn't realise we did,' he shrugged.

'You know you're at pains to let me know you consider me a mere child.'

'I dare not consider you as anything else.'

'Would you like to?'

'*Christy!*' His voice deepened dramatically.

'Here we go again, making fun of me.' She swept around with a toss of her rose-bronze mane.

'What should I do?' Thorne taunted her. 'Sleep with you tonight?'

'Why, have you made some solemn vow you shouldn't?' she cried, a kind of static whipping all around them.

'Have you ever heard of getting in over your head?'

Kit shook her head. 'I'm a great swimmer!'

'You're confusing style with experience.' He caught her wrist, holding her still. 'Calm down, Christy.'

'My calming down depends utterly on you. Why, for instance, is your thumb tracing my veins?'

He suddenly smiled at her. 'Dracula, maybe. I'd love to try it on.'

'Don't smile at me, Thorne Stratton,' she said severely. 'I regard it as destructive.'

'So,' he released her, 'I'll get your present.'

'You didn't have to bother, Thorne,' she said a little breathlessly.

'Christy darling, then why are you so eager?'

'Because I'm sure it's beautiful. You're one man I will trust with impeccable good taste.' Why did he have to excite and confound her with casual endearments?

Kit watched him swing his white-jacketed shoulders, lifting down a long black lacquered box beautifully decorated in swirls of silver and amber and gold and laying it down on the rich burgundy leather-topped desk.

'Can you hear my heart thumping?' she asked huskily.

'Absurdly, I can. Aren't you going to open it?'

She looked down at the box and sucked in her breath. 'I hope this isn't a serious present?'

'It's not a tiara, if that's what you mean!' His topaz eyes gleamed. 'It's a present suitable for a beautiful young girl.'

Kit's slender, long-fingered hands shook slightly. The feeling she was experiencing now she had never felt before. It was as though some new potion was circulating in her blood.

Reverently, she opened up the lid, and there, cushioned in gleaming white satin, were three exquisite young female sculptures made out of ivory and extremely fine gold lacquer. The largest figure was dancing, and her companions were seated in musical poses. They were dressed in the traditional Japanese kimono and obi, and the elaborate hairstyles were secured with perfectly carved tassels and flowers.

For a moment, their beauty and obvious value took her breath away. *'Thorne!'* she gasped.

'I'm glad you like them. Works of art must be treasured.'

'But I can't accept anything so...valuable, and you're not going to tell me they're *not*!'

He shrugged lightly. 'Let's say, when I bought them—at little more than your age—they weren't as valuable as they are now. I fell in love with them, and as soon as I thought of your birthday I made the connection. We share the same powerful love of beauty. I want you to have them, Christiana. You may keep them in custody for your own little girl, but you can't give them away or sell them.'

'As if I would!' Her eyes brilliant, Kit's fingers curled around the dancing figure. 'Isn't she exquisite?'

'Magical.' He gazed down at her bent head. 'The custom-made box is itself a work of art.'

'In fact, it would make a perfect jewel box. If I had any jewels,' she added humorously. 'Thank you so much, Thorne. I shall treasure such a beautiful gift all my life. No one has made quite the same fuss over me before. I think I might go to pieces under your eyes.' In fact, there was a quiver to her full, delicate lips.

Very gently, he took her face into his hands, and with great deliberation touched his mouth to her own—just the merest brush, yet it had a violent joy to it. The very air seemed charged with an unbearable excitement. Since the moment she had met him, Kit had been waiting and watching for something to happen. Yearning overcame her, an intoxicating surge of desire. As he moved his head back, she slipped her arms around his neck, staring up at him with huge, challenging eyes.

'Will you *please* kiss me properly?'

'I'm not totally insane.' Everything that earlier had seemed taut to the point of snapping had been transformed into a relaxed, golden charm. Paradise suited him, and against his burnished tan his mocking eyes were a pure, brilliant topaz.

'Give me *some* credit.' Kit was trembling with her own bravado.

'Christy,' Thorne said indulgently, 'you have the mouth of an enchantress.'

'Kid's stuff, I know.' Instantly, there was temper in her beautifully boned body.

'Haven't you ever heard there's a Mr Right and a Mr Wrong?'

'Yes,' she replied with stung flippancy. 'Is that supposed to stop me from wanting a little excitement? I've refused a dozen invitations to come here.'

'You're an audacious little witch! Just the kind to paint yourself into a corner.' Indolence turned to a coiled power and he spun her so she came up against a ceiling-high cabinet of books. 'You want to be kissed?' he threatened gently.

She stared back at him, her vivid face flushed with daring. 'Yes, and this time put some effort into it!'

'You won't quit, will you?' He made a low growl, like a sleek leopard, deep in his throat.

'All my life I seem to have been travelling towards this point,' Kit said quietly.

'My dear God!' He drew her towards him, one arm powerfully encircling her supple body, the other cradling the back of her head, his long-fingered hand buried deep in her luxuriant mane. Passion roared like a flame. Kit opened up her mouth instinctively, like a thirsting flower, and he crushed her full, delicate lips—yes, *crushed* them. Their teeth grazed, then his tongue stole hers away.

Her spine turned to liquid and her breasts tingled with an urgent fullness. This was too terrible for pleasure. She could feel the heavy throbbing ache in her veins.

'Had enough?'

His warm, clean breath was in her nostrils, and as she drew a tearing sigh his mouth began to travel slowly from the indented corner of her cushiony lips along the sensitive, upraised borders. It was mind-bending in its voluptuousness. In a moment, her legs would buckle under her.

'I must pay you back,' she whispered with fantastic daring, her inhibitions disintegrating in the supercharged heat. She caught his roving, exploring mouth with her own, taking nibbling little bites of his beautiful sculptured mouth. Everything about him was so excitingly perfect to her. She could accept anything he did. Her heart overflowed with a frightening, exhilarating longing. She loved him—yes, *loved* him. His great charm and his stern authority. She even loved his Pommy, patrician voice.

Their chemical interaction was phenomenal, a state of affairs which Thorne apparently found a nightmare and a rapture. He was trying to unwrap her adventurous arms, his efforts rendered token by the immense excitement in the air. Passion had a momentum of its own, crushing everything in its path.

He held her high beneath the breasts, hauling her even closer as her head lolled back.

'This is fantastic!' she panted, seizing a breath. 'Someone might come in.'

'You're acquiring some very bad habits, Christy. Do you need an additional turn-on?'

'I mean, we should wrap it up.'

'When I'm ready.' The playful wrestling had an undercurrent of sexual violence. The suave coolness was gone from his voice and he sounded quite different—a disturbing, dangerous, profoundly exciting man. Her delicate nipples, the soft pink of a young girl, dragged against the glowing silk jacquard and he turned his thumbs so they teased the perfect, conical peaks.

Kit's senses were in turmoil.

'Please, stop, Thorne,' she begged in abrupt alarm. His hands carried an electric current that had her writhing for release.

'I thought you wanted more.'

'I doubted you'd be so...so...'

'Demanding? Think about it, please.'

'You'll have me *screaming*, for God's sake!'

There was a brilliant, responsive gleam in his eyes. 'All eyes and mouth and glorious, untamable hair. Dressing just for me. I could peel that top away. Don't stop me.'

'I *will* stop you.' She reverted in an instant to outraged virgin, trying to bring her fists down on his chest, but he effortlessly held her arms.

'It's a lesson, Christy. *Shut up!*'

'Shut up?' Her eyes widened incredulously and she flung up her head in a high state of passion.

'I may be your lover some time in the future, but not now. You have too much catching up to do. I'm your friend, always.'

'Some friend!' Kit began to rub her slender arms.

'I didn't hurt you,' he snapped. 'Damn it, I feel guilty even kissing you!'

'And I *will* provoke you, won't I?' She sounded worried, pushing back her tumbled hair and adjusting her wide sash.

'My dear girl, you relish the challenge.'

'How can I learn if I don't have the best teacher?'

He looked down at her, half-way between a uniquely male hostility and unwilling admiration. 'You're really something, you know that?' he said softly.

Kit's beautiful eyes lit up with a youthful elation. 'Your life could use change. When you first came here you were unbearably tense. You frightened me, you looked so keyed up and severe. You'd seen terrible things and you'd suffered. It left its mark. It must have been shocking to watch horror and bloodshed at close quarters. Your time here has healed you. Maybe even I have helped you. Instead of being desperate about staying alive, you only have to be desperate about fending off *me*.'

'You wicked, bold girl!' Thorne bent his head briefly and kissed her mouth. 'Let's move.'

'Shall I take my present or leave it here until I leave?'

'Leave it. We'll collect it later.'

'Thank you again for such a wonderful gift.' Kit flung a quick look into a japanned mirror that hung over a brass-bound Korean cabinet. 'Oh, goodness!' she recoiled.

'You look great,' he assured her.

The uncompromising bluntness surprised her and she turned, to question his judgement. 'I don't know about that. I look...'

'Sexually aroused?'

'Well, yes,' she flushed.

'Try to think of sober things,' he suggested without mockery.

'Alyce Schaffer?' Her beautiful eyes flashed upwards. 'There must be something in your relationship worth protecting?'

'Christy!' Thorne shook his burnished gold head and his eyes glinted.

'How brash of me! I'm celebrating my twentieth birthday, yet I'm asking impertinent questions.'

'All that's important for you to believe is that twenty is too young for me,' said Thorne seriously.

'Suppose I were not a virgin? Would that change your mind?'

Lights in his topaz eyes flickered, but he shook his head. 'Don't do anything rash just for me.'

'Purely a hypothetical question. There must be some basis for your fear of me,' she pointed out limpidly.

'Christy, Christy, the risks you take!' He moved one arm to snake around her waist, and as he did so the door almost burst open after only a token rap.

Alyce Schaffer stood in the doorway, her whole attitude bringing to mind the actions of a highly suspicious spouse. Her light blue eyes glittered, rivalling the *paillettes* on her slinky designer dress—it must have taken her hours to dress—and her fine regular features were tight and ominous. It came as a considerable shock to Kit, who was expecting brimstone and fire, to hear her voice emerge very mildly indeed.

'Ah, there you are!' she announced, as if sure their reaction would be gracious. 'I've been looking for you everywhere.'

'Perhaps this is where you left your specs?' Kit swung around obligingly, looking towards the desk.

'My goodness, what wit!' trilled Alyce. 'A smart girl like you, Miss Lacey, should find better things to do with her time.'

'You needn't tell me!' Kit smiled and threw up her hands. 'You want to talk to Thorne. This really is a treat, to be invited to the study. I'll cut along.'

'That's right, dear,' Alyce cooed. 'Actually, you'd best get outside. The Senator has been asking a lot of questions about you.'

'I expect he'll suggest I go into a life of politics.'

'You stir up a brew of trouble as it is,' Thorne murmured mildly. 'Why don't we *all* go out and see what it is the Senator wants to know?'

In fact, the Senator was only tantalised by a feeling of familiarity. 'I don't understand it, Miss Lacey,' he said jovially, 'but I've seen your double someplace.'

'They do say we've all got one,' Thorne commented, and deftly steered the conversation into other channels. One didn't have to be acute to realise that the redirection was deliberate.

'What the heck's going on?' demanded Glenn over the lavish supper. 'Who *is* it you bring to mind?'

'I was having rather a serious discussion with Lady Eliot,' Melly told Kit almost worriedly. 'In the nicest way possible, she wanted to know all about me, or, if I'm going to be accurate, all about *you*. You weren't snatched from somebody else's cradle, were you? Remember that film we saw on TV about the wrong babies being given to the new mothers? A mix-up at the hospital. It was *true*, too!' Melly's lovely porcelain face looked dismayed and Kit, loving her, burst out protectively.

'Oh, don't be silly, Melly! How could you ever doubt, even for a second, that we're sisters?'

'Of course we are!' Melly stared into Kit's eyes. 'But look at our hair. Look at our eyes. Look at our skin!'

'Are you nuts?' Kit, who had been feeling hungry, suddenly put down her plate. 'Plenty of families have children who don't resemble each other in the least. Look at the Kellys. There are six of them and no two look alike.'

'But they either look like their mother or father or a cross between each,' Glenn offered almost apologetically. 'I don't understand the least thing about genes. Wasn't it in that show that one of the kids had dark eyes? Two blue-eyed parents can't have a child with brown eyes?'

'Hey, this is a party!' Kit said, almost wrathfully. 'Let's have some light conversation. I don't intend to spend the rest of the night trying to figure out who it is I vaguely resemble.'

'Between the two of us,' Glenn joked, 'I think it's Helen of Troy. Was she a redhead?'

Despite her apparent interest, Kit had no direct conversation with Lady Eliot until shortly before that distinguished lady retired for bed.

'Come and sit with me for a moment.' She raised a thin, elegant arm towards Kit as she was circling that particular conversation area. 'Your sister Melanie is a delightful young woman. Come and tell me a little about *you*.'

'I'd be dearly grateful, Lady Eliot,' Kit returned softly, 'if you'd tell me why you want to know.'

'I don't understand, my dear.' Lady Eliot watched Kit carefully, her still brilliant eyes hooded.

'I think you do.' Always one to take the initiative, Kit sat down on the sofa and looked directly but respectfully into the elderly woman's eyes. 'I remind you of someone, don't I? Someone who meant a great deal to you. Someone who is no longer with you. Someone who may have hurt you very badly.'

Shockingly, Lady Eliot spread the thin fingers of her hand across her breast, as though a sudden pain had squeezed her heart.

'I'm sorry—are you all right?' Kit placed her hand on Lady Eliot's other arm, realising *her* heart was pounding too. 'Forgive me, I've upset you.' She now felt a wave of distress and remorse. No one knew better how forthright she was. It had been drummed into her all her life, to no effect.

But Lady Eliot could not speak. She sat, slumped, her habitual regal carriage clearly impossible.

'Dear God!' Kit stared desperately around the room, gasping aloud with relief as Thorne entered from an outside deck and crossed immediately to them as if he knew the extraordinary intensity of the situation.

'What is it? You're not well?' He dropped down beside Lady Eliot, taking her hand, his voice charged with concern.

'Nothing, my boy. Nothing.' Yet Lady Eliot leaned against him, obviously grateful for his strength. 'I'm sorry I've upset your little friend, I'll explain it to her at another time.'

'I'll take you to your room,' Thorne said with quiet decision, catching Kit's eye and obviously dismissing her.

Kit sprang to her feet with tears in her eyes. 'Please forgive *me*, Lady Eliot. It's I who have upset you. It was never my intention—please believe that. My mother deeply regrets my impetuous ways.'

'Your *mother*!' Lady Eliot put a shaking hand to her eyes, as though she found that especially difficult. 'I'll talk to you again, my dear. I *cannot* now.'

Kit fled.

So intent was she on reaching Glenn and Melly that she didn't even notice Alyce Schaffer glaring at her until that resolute lady grasped her tightly by the arm.

'Stop what you're doing now,' she said bitingly, just below her breath. 'Stop it now—I'm serious!'

'Not tonight, Mrs Schaffer.' Kit threw the other woman's restraining hand off.

'No one talks like that to me!' Alyce held her wineglass as if she intended to fling the contents into Kit's face.

'Believe me, lady, if you start something, I'll take it up,' Kit responded instantly to the challenge. 'Who do you think you are, stalking around after me?'

'The way you're going after Thorne isn't healthy,' Alyce accused her with a look of offence.

'The only way you're going to be able to convince me of that is to tell me he's my uncle,' retorted Kit.

'Do me a favour, and drop all that flip talk,' Alyce snapped tautly. 'You're embarrassing him. Surely you realise that?'

'Why berate me? Surely a sophisticated lady like you should know better than to break down study doors?'

'Thorne and I have an understanding,' Alyce declared flatly. 'Both of us come and go as we please, but we never break up.'

'Does your companion know this?' asked Kit.

Alyce shrugged. 'My dear, we come from a different world, one you wouldn't understand. One, I venture, you will never enter. Thorne and I will probably be discussing you in bed tonight. I could just say I've had a little chat with you, pointing out how much you're embarrassing him with your schoolgirl chasing, and you'll just stop. We all have to get a hold on ourselves at different times. Go out and discover someone your own age. I do know what I'm talking about. By the way,' she added, 'your boyfriend has really been enjoying himself with your sister. I think he's just found out she's a lot prettier than you.'

'A lot nicer, too.' Kit didn't even bother to hide her anger. 'Step out of the way or you'll get a punch in the nose!'

'You really ought to learn to control yourself at social functions,' Alyce sneered, but she no longer blocked the doorway. 'Just remember, my dear, what you'll never have, I have now!'

'What are you looking so wild-eyed about?' Melly demanded as Kit reached their side.

'Yeah, what's eating you, Kit?' Glenn looked around them almost belligerently. 'Has someone been saying something to you?'

'Now you're getting it,' fumed Kit. 'Honestly, that Schaffer woman is one nasty female!'

Melly nodded sagely. 'You're threatening her, that's why.'

'And how's that?' Kit edged them back against the balustrade, unwilling that the other guests should overhear them.

'It's obvious she's got the hots for Stratton.'

'Glenn, what a terrible expression!' Melly stared at him.

'Sorry, love, but some things keep rolling off my tongue,' he apologised.

'Not in the company of a little angel.' For the first time, Kit smiled.

'She's nuts about him,' Glenn said.

'How could she not be?' Melly sighed. 'He's the most gorgeous, beautiful man!'

'How I envy him,' said Glenn wryly.

'You have no need to be jealous, Glenn,' Melly answered quickly, sounding as if she meant it.

'Anyway, she just told me they're lovers,' Kit announced shortly.

'Invariably, one is with one's girlfriends,' Glenn laughed.

'*Is* she?' Kit demanded, staring him straight in the eye. 'You're a man—treacherous sex.'

For an instant, Glenn's own jealousy got the better of him. 'Of course she is, sweetie,' he said laconically. 'Nothing wrong in it, is there? If she didn't look so hard, she'd positively wow them. Not that I suppose she's like that in bed. I'm sure they're lovers. You've only got to see them together.'

Kit's anger faded as quickly as it had come. 'Of course,' she said bleakly. 'If I had any sense at all, I'd stay right away from here.'

'So we'll go,' Glenn offered instantly. 'We'll drop Melly off, then I'll take you home.'

'Home?' Kit felt an abrupt surge of sadness. 'Where *is* home for me?'

'Kit!' Melly put her arm around her sister as if she would protect her. 'I'll stay with you.'

'Mother would go out of her mind.'

'Yes, she would,' Melly said broodingly. 'Even the best mothers can be wrong.'

They all walked around quickly, saying their good-nights. Thorne had not reappeared, and Kit knew she couldn't leave without hearing how Lady Eliot was, otherwise she would gladly have forgotten her manners. She was madly in love with Thorne. Thorne and Alyce Schaffer were lovers. *She* was a complete fool. Maybe she could be forgiven because she was only twenty.

Sickeningly, Bart Madden kissed her on the mouth, not appearing to notice Kit's quick, angry reaction. She flung her head back, her violet eyes locked on his in disgust. The kiss had been wet and open—an insult, she thought fierily.

'It's been a long night, hasn't it?' he drawled. 'Alyce is a very possessive woman.'

'You sound as though you admire her?'

He smiled. Not a pleasant smile. 'No. I *do* admire you.'

Kit didn't deign to answer, but as she went to swing away he caught her arm. 'Come now, don't act so offended. You're a very beautiful girl.'

'I think of myself first as a human being. You wouldn't dream of taking liberties with another man,' she retorted.

'Heavens, I should hope not!' He gave an exaggerated roll of his dark eyes.

'You know perfectly well what I mean.'

'And what do we have here, a young feminist?'

'You bet your life you do! I detest men who treat women like goods on display—usually for them. You had no right to kiss me, even on the cheek. I very much resented being kissed on the mouth. I found it offensive.'

'Then, my dear, allow me to apologise. I simply didn't know your mettle.'

'A true gentleman is not a man of calculation. A real man knows how to respect women.'

'What you need is a real man,' he told her with a narrow smile, his near-black eyes touching insolently on her breasts and legs. 'I'm staying on for a few days. Perhaps we could meet?'

'I think not, Mr Madden.' Kit's luscious, full-lipped mouth curled contemptuously.

'You may change your mind. I know exactly how to take care of you.'

Kit turned away in a rage. It was terrible to be rendered powerless by convention. What she really felt like was taking a sock at him. Maybe she should have been born a boy!

Senator Gower shook her hand. 'We'll meet again, Miss Lacey, I'm sure.' He wasn't being social; he looked as if he fully anticipated her entry into his ambit.

'Where's Thorne?' Melly asked breathlessly. 'We can't go without saying goodnight to him. I had a marvellous time. Everyone was so *nice* to me!'

Just as they thought Thorne would never appear, he walked through to the living-room, his handsome face taut. His eyes locked for an immeasurable instant with Kit's.

'Is Lady Eliot all right?' Without knowing it, Kit had the palms of her hands locked together.

'I stayed with her for a while. She's strong.'

'Is there something we should know?' Melly asked anxiously. 'Did Lady Eliot take ill?'

'Not at all.' Thorne put a calming hand on Melly's shoulder. 'She thought it best to retire.'

'I was worried.' Kit stared up at Thorne without moving. 'It was something I said, wasn't it?'

'Unconsciously, Christy,' Thorne said quietly.

'I knew it!' Her brilliant eyes glittered with tears. 'I was admiring her so much, yet in the end I upset her.'

'But how?' Glenn asked almost fiercely, and put his arm around Kit's shoulder. 'You're the last person in this world to upset an old lady!'

'I agree,' Melly announced stoutly. 'Whatever happened?'

'Everyone has a vulnerable spot,' Thorne explained. 'We must presume that Kit reached Lady Eliot at the deepest level. It's not the time to consider it now.'

'I don't think I'll sleep tonight,' said Kit.

'Then stay here.'

'Goodness, Kit, come home with me. Daddy hates you in that place, anyway.'

Kit shook her glowing mane. 'It's all right—really, Melly. I couldn't bear to be under the same roof as Alyce Schaffer.'

'And why, particularly, is that?' Thorne looked searchingly at Kit.

'Are you asking me to betray a confidence?' She threw up her head in a now familiar challenging attitude.

'If you'll wait a few moments,' he returned rather crisply, 'I'll drive you home. Glenn will be going out of his way if he has to drop Melly.'

'No problem,' Glenn insisted.

'I want to talk to Kit, anyway.' Thorne's firm statement had the effect of deterring Glenn from his plan. He had always wanted to be Kit's hero, yet he felt his valour fade against Stratton's sheer power. But then the man was a real hero, Glenn thought dismally. He had the stamp of a man who had endured great pain and danger and somehow come through it with his integrity intact. It was incredibly difficult to fight him.

Melly drew herself up and kissed her taller sister on her warm, flushed cheek. 'See you tomorrow,' she whispered consolingly, unable to hide an inner excitement in her large, luminous eyes. 'It was a wonderful party, Thorne,' she told him. 'Thank you for inviting me. It means I'm grown up. I hope Lady Eliot has a good night. She was very nice to me, even if I felt she was really trying to learn all about Kit. Imagine that! Anyone would think there was a connection.'

Kit's chin lifted. 'Impossible!' she flared. Every emotion she felt was reflected in her face, and there for all to see was a mounting tension and anxiety. Some terrible truth lay buried—a truth that, were it not for

Thorne, might never come to light. She realised in her panic that she wanted no secrets to be revealed. Secrets had a way of hurting people. If she only dared think about it, she had been hurt enough.

CHAPTER EIGHT

BARELY a word was spoken all the way home in the car. Tensions sharp as rapiers were flashing dangerously. Finally, Kit spoke as Thorne drew the Jaguar up in front of the small contemporary bungalow that overlooked the bay. It was hidden from view by an exotic flourish of tropical planting, as were the more imposing residences of the neighbours.

'Just how well do you know Lady Eliot?' Kit demanded in a voice husky with emotion.

He took her up sharply. 'Not terribly well. I've met her on and off over the years. I knew her brother a lot better. He used to be the High Commissioner in London, Sir Andrew Sinclair. Lady Eliot's late husband was in the same business as my father. He held many important diplomatic posts. You understand how our lives might become entwined?'

'Of course I do,' she said shortly. 'What I don't understand is what Lady Eliot has to do with me? I wanted to ask but couldn't. As soon as I...'

'...challenged her?'

'...she became visibly distressed. I think what I was saying was quite ordinary.'

'Ordinary for you. Shall we get out, Christy? I want to see you safely into the house.'

'I can check myself,' she blurted childishly. The closer she got to him, the more she lost all sense of herself. All sorts of emotions were stirring in her body, not the least of it a hot flush of antagonism made more unbearable by the sexuality behind it. She knew he desired her, but he was a man who would not commit himself. It was humiliating and destructive, and she had only herself to blame.

She flounced out of the car and he caught her up as she reached the door. 'Don't you think you should leave an outside light on?' he said drily.

'Perhaps you can tell me what's wrong with the switch?' she returned sweetly.

'It won't work?'

'That's just what I mean.'

'Why are you so angry?'

Kit unlocked the door quickly and darted into the house. 'Well now, Thorne, thank you so much for seeing me home. If you don't want to check under the bed I'll say goodnight.'

'Relax, relax,' he said coolly. 'I *will* check under the bed, Christy. It's just a feeling I have.'

'I don't need a Big Brother!'

'One would have to feel sorry for the poor guy.' He moved with his lithe, elegant stride across the living-room and into the bedroom, while Kit tried ineffectually to control the faint hysteria that was welling in her. 'Anyone with a serious thought for security would have a screen on these windows.' He lifted the long curtains back and peered out into the fragrant night.

'Who needs security around here? I have good neighbours.'

'You haven't a clue what you are talking about.' Thorne jerked the shutters in and switched on the ceiling fan. 'There's far too much dense vegetation around this house. This area might be paradise, but it *does* have snakes.'

'Mostly harmless. I'm sure you fuss too much about me. I'm not at all nervous. The neighbours are in screeching distance, as you know.'

'I'll get the light on the porch fixed.' He glanced at her briefly before leaving the room.

'Paddy said he'll do it.'

'Then Paddy should get on with it.'

'Don't *talk* about my father, Thorne!' Kit was so agitated, she hit out at him as he passed.

'My feelings of sensibility have somehow got lost. What are you doing here, Kit? It chills my bones to think of you here on your own. You have a family. What would make your father allow you to go?'

'Why in hell do you think?' She couldn't endure being near him and not in his arms. She almost literally lost her senses, swaying towards him with one small clenched fist upraised. 'My mother doesn't *want* me. The woman I call Clare doesn't want me. She has trouble allowing me to call her Mother. Maybe it's a classic case—the textbooks are full of weird complexes.'

'Come here to me.' He enfolded her shaking body in his arms and she turned her head like a child along his chest. 'You've told Paddy how you feel?'

'Of course I've told Paddy. You don't think he's happy?'

'How could he be happy, the way he's living?'

'You have reasons for everything you do, Thorne,' Kit twisted her head back to look up at him. 'What have you been speaking to Paddy about? You don't tell me, but other people know. What's Lady Eliot doing here? Something about me struck her to the heart, I'm sure of it, Thorne. Don't fob me off with that cool British stuff—I saw the evidence of my own eyes.'

'So you reminded her of someone. When she wants to, she'll let you know.'

She stared up at him for a long time, loving and hating the impenetrable façade. 'You *won't* tell me, will you?'

'I don't know that there is anything *to* tell,' he said maddeningly, lifting one hand and pushing the deep shining waves from her face. 'This is best discussed with your father.'

'Is it possible my self-appointed Big Brother is trying to frighten me?' she demanded, her eyes almost purple with emotion. 'There's nothing to tell, but go and discuss it with your father. How can I not help feeling wretched and confused? You brought Lady Eliot here, didn't you?'

'My dear child, she came with the Senator.'

'That's a bit thick!' Kit gave a brittle little laugh. 'God, I hate that English impassiveness. You're right in the middle of this, Thorne.'

'There isn't anything I wouldn't do for you, Christy,' he said, almost without expression. 'Leave all your emotions alone for a bit.' Abruptly he released her. 'I've trapped your father a couple of times into conversation, he appears to have dissociated himself almost entirely from the past. It's almost impossible to get him to talk about anything.'

'So, what are you insinuating? Something *unspeakable*?' The blood drained from beneath her beautiful skin and her eyes almost swallowed her face.

'Christy,' he said curtly, 'why must you over-dramatise every situation?'

Kit returned the curtness in full measure, moving towards him like an avenging angel. 'Why would I ever want to fall in love with you? You're trying to ruin my life!'

'Stop talking like an idiot,' he said bitingly. 'You want to rusticate, do you? You want to hide away in some little corner? You, with your beauty and character, and a talent you haven't even begun to explore. What about your painting? Some people think such God-given gifts must be used. Do you think you're not answerable? Do you think all you have to give to life is a small competence? You have an advanced intelligence and a gift that no amount of money can acquire. Your duty, Christy, is to expand, not hide.'

'With what consequences?' she shouted. 'You know a great deal more than you're telling me. Is there no one I can turn to? I've never known security in my life. Do you realise that?' She shook helplessly, looking so young and vulnerable that it pushed him beyond endurance. His initial gesture of comfort, so protective at the beginning, changed abruptly in character as Kit refused, like a rejected child, to accept him passively.

'Who's my *doppelgänger*, Thorne? *You* know.' Kit fought his strong, restraining arms for no other reason than to find release. There was actual satisfaction in unleashing primitive aggressions. She enjoyed beating at him with her hands, her anger strengthened by a powerful, sensual component. There was gratification in having him subdue her, a subtle love-play rivalling the fiery impulse.

'Please stop, Christy,' he begged her.

A hero *begging*?

'I *told* you to go!' she snapped.

The twist to his mouth was more pronounced, brackets scored deeply into his fine golden skin. 'This is madness, and you know it,' he muttered.

'I associate madness with you. You've shown me the meaning of being a woman.'

'I won't *do* this!'

Kit drew in her breath and bit hard on her lip in a vain attempt to control herself. The anger was all gone and in its place was a profound need. It crushed her with its weight.

'Oh, Thorne,' she said brokenly, 'love me.' Such sadness beset her, she crumpled against him, burrowing like a child for comfort.

'Christy.' He folded her to him with such tenderness that tears flooded her eyes.

'I feel I've lived in a shadow world. You're the only one who's real.'

'Hush.' He smoothed the glowing weight of her hair, the hard angle of his jawline resting on the top of her head. The compassion on his face was arresting, the expression of a man who knew and understood suffering.

'I'm embarrassing you, aren't I,' sighed Kit. 'Alyce Schaffer said I was. Terrible, isn't it? You're the hero of my dreams.'

'It seems to me you should meet a lot of men. I'm no hero, Christy. I'm an ordinary man, trying to do the best job he can.'

'That's what makes you a hero. It's the striving. Don't blame me too much if I've fallen in love with you. Put it down to late adolescence.'

'Here, sit with me for a moment.' Thorne bore them both backwards, settling himself in a deep armchair and cradling her affectionately. 'All this trauma will pass. Your family conflicts will be resolved. You have to be strong, Christy. You *are* strong.'

'No, I'm not. At least, not all the time.' She gave a choked little hiccough. 'You really like me, Thorne, don't you?'

'You know I do.' His voice deepened, but he scrupulously avoided looking into her eyes, or stroking her satin skin.

'Would you call me hard and aggressive?'

'About as hard as a ten-month-old baby. I think the angelic Melly would be more determined about getting her own way.'

'My mother loves Melly. We all do. The great mystery is, why doesn't everyone love *me*? I wouldn't have thought I was a difficult person. Perhaps I'm a bit outspoken.'

'Make Patrick talk to you,' Thorne said.

'He hasn't done anything wrong, has he?' Kit tipped her head back against his shoulder and raised her drowning eyes.

'No, little one!'

'So why do I feel so threatened? There are so many disturbing undercurrents. They've always been there, an undeniable fact of life.'

'Tomorrow is Sunday. Why don't you ask your father to come and visit you?'

'He *is* coming.' Kit stared at him with huge eyes. 'What is Paddy supposed to tell me?'

'What time?' There was a frown between Thorne's arched golden-brown eyebrows.

'In the morning.'

'I'll call down,' he said quietly, though his amber eyes were burning. 'It might help if I'm here.'

'Help *what*?' Desperately, Kit pushed up and even put her two hands to his face.

'To try and talk things out,' he said evasively.

'It seems to me, there's nothing to talk about. We've unearthed the fact that Clare doesn't want me. It's been pretty well buried all these years.'

'You have a career, a whole life in front of you. I'm directing my efforts towards seeing that happen.'

'And what has Lady Eliot to do with this?' Kit asked.

'Perhaps she just arrived at a dramatic moment?' The taut, handsome face was composed and unreadable.

'You don't have to lie to me, Thorne,' she said quietly.

'My dear, what evidence is there that I am? I'm trying to help you, but I can't cause too much interference in your life. Now, I think you've had enough for one night. It must be time for bed.'

'Yes, Uncle Thorne,' she said miserably.

'And let's leave it like that.' His beautiful, chiselled mouth curved in self-mockery.

'I won't bother you any more,' she promised.

Already withdrawing, he seemed to hesitate a moment. 'Don't be silly, Christy. I want you to bother me.'

'I can get along without an uncle!' She spoke angrily, though she was trying to control her tears.

'Don't cry, Christy. I'm not worth your tears.'

'Of course you're not worth my tears,' she said furiously. 'What man is? Paddy has lied to me all my life— for sure, I don't know in what way, but I have the feeling I'm bound to find out. Now, you don't have to bounce me on your knee...'

'In another minute I'll put you over it...'

'How else could you get the better of me?' she flared at him.

'Like this. The thing that betrays us both.' Thorne angled her trembling body into the crook of his arm and, though her struggles didn't stop, took possession of her mouth and made it his own.

She lay there for a long time while he drained the very soul from her body, his hand smoothing, tormenting her breasts, fingertips moving urgently over the deep naked V but not moving the lustrous turquoise fabric aside.

The intensity that was in him pulsed from her as well, as extreme as lightning flashing over their heads.

Kit didn't move, *couldn't*, since his strength and aggression were so vastly superior, but neither was she shrinking from his fearful male power. She was confronting it with a femaleness that had him almost devouring her, so when she gave a little moan he understood it as a sign of triumph, almost throwing her off.

'What's important,' he said rigidly as he brought them both to their feet, 'is that we get your life straightened out. Every time we're alone together there's always the danger of going too far. Ultimately, Christy, I won't be able to cope with your woman magic. You don't seem to have a clue about turning violence on yourself. What you feel for me I've taken as infatuation, something inevitable at twenty and something you'll get over. You're infinitely desirable—I can't tell you you're not. What I *can* tell you is that I believe in protecting the rights of vulnerable young women. If you were even four or five years old I wouldn't have a qualm about picking you up and taking you to bed. But you represent, to me, innocence. You're even as direct as a child. I want you to know exactly what you're getting into. If I make love to you, it won't be a little girl's fantasy. So far, I've only kissed you. Sex is a different level. It involves giving your whole body. To *me*.'

'Is that something evil?' Kit wanted to hurt him as he was hurting her.

'It's something absolutely crucial to your happiness, something neither of us might be able to overcome. I'm a moral man, Christy. If I weren't, I would eat you up.' His eyes were glittery now, his mouth thinned, his jaw hard.

'All right, Thorne,' she said shakily, and pushed the auburn-rose mass off her shoulders. 'From tonight, I'm going to practise self-denial. Evidently, I haven't been following your high moral code. I'll get cracking on modesty as well. You may not believe this, but up until now I've been carrying it to Puritan extremes. I'll re-

nounce you like a little saint. I know you're thinking it's
infatuation at my stage in life, but some people find real
love early. You underestimate me when you think I can't
make the distinction. Still, I have my pride. I've been
told you've reached a high level of understanding with
Alyce Schaffer. On her own admission, she gets pretty
close to the action. And, just so it's not wrong, she's a
widow as well. You'll be able to vent your dangerous
passions on *her*!' Kit turned and fled into her bedroom,
slamming the door. A minute or so later, the smooth-
engined Jaguar roared away, and in an excess of passion
Kit picked up a small ornament and hurled it at the wall.

Don't love me, was what he meant!

From long habit, Kit rose early next morning and cycled
down to the bay for her early morning swim. The
bungalow wasn't far from the bay, but just the same she
missed the wonderful convenience of having the blue
water at her doorstep. She wondered about Melly and
Glenn. She wondered why she had never thought about
Mell's championing Glenn on all possible occasions; she
had always taken it as an extension of her own view.
But Melly really cared about Glenn in her own right.
She had been stimulated last night, not only because she
was exposed to pleasant, sophisticated people in a luxur-
ious setting, but because Glenn had reacted to her. Even
the poisonous Alyce Schaffer had pointed that out. In
her own way, Kit had always thought of Melly as a child,
but Melly was fast growing up. With hindsight, she could
see Melly had been tender-hearted towards Glenn for
quite some time. The truly amazing thing was that
Glenn's tortured parent had reacted positively to Melly's
sweet nature. She, Kit, was taboo, but Melly was seen
as the right sort of friend for Glenn to have. Life was
simply incredible, and it was hardest on women who went
after a future. Maybe she would have been better off if
she actually couldn't *do* anything. Her own mother de-
cried her aims and ambitions.

The water was glorious, invigorating, refreshing. There was no better exercise or relaxation in the world. Afterwards, with her wet hair ribboned down her back, Kit went for a walk, remembering that morning weeks ago when she had first laid eyes on Thorne Stratton. Even then she had surrendered to his magnetism. A powerful instinct told her he was the only man she would ever love. It was no 'accident', his involvement in her life. It was meant to be, and she would have to deal with the pain when he went away. There was little doubt he had brought Lady Eliot to North Queensland for a purpose, but *why* was shrouded in mystery. Perhaps Paddy could solve it. It was time for Paddy to have done with the pretending.

Morning was brilliant, the sea swelling and lifting to a gentle rhythm, the colour indescribable, the air opulent with the warm perfume of flowers. Seagulls walked the beach or burrowed their beaks in the sand, and as Kit's naked feet approached them they gave a running little shuffle, then soared away. The sea was always such an exciting companion. Not a day passed that her ears didn't ring with the chatter of birds; her eyes didn't glory in vast stretches of water and moist rain-forest. It had been the grandest place on earth to grow up in, but now she had to leave and move on. Life was a challenge, and she felt humbled by the knowledge that she had been granted a gift. She *could* paint. Subconsciously, she had sought never to spoil things for Paddy. Paddy was the artist in the family; her talent had been inherited from him. She had never wished to show herself as competitive. Clearly, a child must be second to the parent. But now everything had changed. She had to develop to survive.

Without realising it, Kit found herself walking towards the headland. Once, it had been home. Clare and Paddy had bought her a present for her birthday, and Paddy had promised to bring it over. Poor Paddy! He was like a man split in two. There was no reason why she shouldn't be able to call in on her own family now. After all, they hadn't parted in anger. A terrible sadness, maybe. With such clashes in temperament, there could be no easy way. Clare had obviously struggled with her warring feelings and the need for peace and tranquillity had gained control. Perhaps her abandonment had begun in infancy. Perhaps she was a changeling, after all.

No one met her as she climbed the terraced garden. A lot of the beds were overgrown, she noted. Kit, the gardener, had taken up residence elsewhere. She gave a wry little laugh, quickly stifled. Clare's face was staring at her through the kitchen window and she lifted her arm and waved.

Clare waved back.

Things were easier now they were apart. Kit wondered if it occurred in other families. She supposed it did. Nothing was ever going to turn a stern mother into a laughing friend. It was not as though Clare had been a 'cuddly' mother even with Melly; Clare referred to herself as 'reserved'.

As she padded across the deck to the kitchen, Kit was glad she was wearing a simple one-piece costume. Her mother didn't care for her in her skimpy bikinis, even if her girl friends begged her to make them several of the same. The costume she was wearing was a beautiful orchid pink, cut high to flatter long shapely legs, slashed low to reveal the gentle curves of fresh young breasts. Any skimpy costume suited Kit to perfection; she had a beautiful body.

Kit tried to put her whole heart into her smile, moving into the kitchen where her mother was preparing fresh fruit salad from pawpaws, pineapples, bananas and passionfruit.

'I was hoping you were up,' Kit said brightly, and touched a finger to an arrangement of golden hibiscus.

'How nice to see you, Kit.' Clare returned the smile. 'What about putting the kettle on and we'll have a cup of tea together?'

'Lovely!'

'There's a shift of Melly's hanging behind the bathroom door. You might like to slip it on.'

Despite her best intentions, Kit almost said, yes, Reverend Mother. Why was it that Clare always made her feel disturbingly wanton? Clare had an obsession about flaunting one's body—as though something God-given could be shockingly seductive. It made for anxieties in life.

In the bathroom, Kit slipped Melly's peach and honey-coloured shift over her swimming costume. She was taller than Melly and it made much of her knees. She picked up Melly's comb and dragged it through her salt-tangled hair, watching it spring in a riot of waves and curls around the golden oval of her sun-kissed face. That completed, she went back to the kitchen. Clare, more than anyone, knew how to curb enthusiasm, nevertheless Kit was determined their brief time together would be pleasant.

'Melly was in very late,' Clare told her with characteristic sternness. 'I wish you'd remember that she's my baby.'

'She enjoyed herself,' Kit remarked soothingly, spooning tea-leaves into the pot. 'Everyone said how beautiful she looked.

'Yes, she did, didn't she?' Clare smiled fondly. 'There's such a lovely, open quality about Melly's looks—a sweet wholesomeness. Though I'd been waiting and waiting, I actually missed you when you came home. I expect Glenn dropped you off after? I hope you realise, Kit, it wouldn't do to ask him in. You didn't, did you?'

Kit felt a sudden chill. 'No, Mum.' If she said Melly had come home alone with Glenn it would have led to a lecture.

'There's no point whatever in encouraging Glenn. He's a nice boy—one can't help admiring him—but he will always do what his mother wants. He owes it to her.'

Kit knew better than to argue, when once she might have. Glenn owed his mother love and consideration; he did not owe her his life.

'I hope you're listening, Kit,' Clare cautioned.

'I'm not interested in Glenn, Clare, you know that. I hope he'll always be my friend, but my feeling for him is sisterly. Melly is far more interested in him than I am.'

'Melly's still a child.'

No, she isn't, Mother.

The electric kettle came quickly to the boil and Kit poured on the water. 'Can I help you there?' she asked.

'No, thanks—almost through. You know how your father likes a fruit compôte in the morning.'

'OK if we have toast?'

'Of course, dear. This is still your home, Kit. You may do as you please,' Clare told her.

Except live here.

Kit moved competently around the kitchen, setting the breakfast things up. 'I had such an extraordinary experience last night,' she began conversationally.

'How you do dramatise, Kit!' Clare said with smiling irritation. 'It marks you, the way you speak.'

'Do you *want* to hear what happened?'

'Certainly, dear,' Clare looked up, surveying Kit with her cool grey eyes. 'I'm all ears.' She went back to her chopping up of the pineapple.

'Have you ever heard of a woman called Lady *Eliot*?'

Clare's hand seemed to slip, and the index finger began to trickle blood.

'Oh, goodness, you've cut your hand!' Kit cried in dismay, and looked about urgently for a paper towel.

'Leave me,' muttered Clare in a shaky voice.

'Show it to me, Mum. I don't think it's deep.'

'I said, *leave me*!'

The ambivalence that was in Clare, what Kit thought of as a mixture of love and hate, had one direction only.

'Why, you *hate* me!' Kit exclaimed in a stunned, bewildered voice. 'What have I ever done to you that you should hate me?'

'Would you like to know?' Clare cried distractedly, picking up a roll of paper towelling and wrenching a strip off. Her finger was bleeding profusely now, and she was reacting as though it were a mortal wound. 'The woman you call Lady Eliot? Well, my dear, she's your *grandmother*!'

'*No!*' The strangled little protest died in Kit's throat. She sat down heavily in a kitchen chair before her legs went from under her.

'What do you think has caused the turmoil all these years? Why did your father abandon everything and come up here? What do you think was the reason?'

'Lady Eliot is his *mother*?'

'God, Kit, you're a fool!' Clare's pale, good-looking face contorted with old griefs.

'She's *your* mother?' The healthy flush of blood had faded from Kit's cheeks.

'Have another guess!' Clare gave a wild laugh.

'I don't have to guess, Clare,' Kit said with dreadful calm. 'You owe it to me to tell me the truth. Even as a little child, a four-year-old, I had no true sense of identity. Our relationship has never been good. Whatever happened to you and Paddy that made things so difficult?'

'Ask your father,' Clare suggested in a hard, flat voice, drooping her shoulders like a woman many years older.

'I'm asking my *mother*,' Kit said sternly, fixing her great eyes on Clare's working face.

'Your mother's dead!' Clare cried in a voice that riveted Kit to the seat. 'Your terrible, beautiful mother is *dead*. But she's haunted us. My God, has she haunted us!'

'You're mad!' Kit suddenly shouted, and leapt to her feet. 'Your mind has snapped!'

'Why wouldn't it, the cross I've borne all these years?'

'*Me*, I'm the cross?' Kit's heart was pounding so violently she could hardly breathe.

'What's going on here?' demanded Paddy, coming into the kitchen. 'You're shouting so much, you woke me up!'

'Who's Lady Eliot, Paddy?' Kit turned terrible eyes on him.

'So he brought her here, did he? I never thought he would.' From the expression on Paddy's face, one would have thought his doctor had told him he was about to die.

'Paddy——' Kit rushed to her father and grasped his arm. 'You're destroying me! Do you know that? *Who* is Lady Eliot?'

'One of two people in the world I had to keep you from.'

'Why don't you take your daughter off and tell her the whole story?' Clare cried raggedly, the tears pouring down her face.

'I'm not Clare's daughter, am I?'

'Good work, Kit,' Clare laughed hysterically, and without any hesitation Patrick moved forward and slapped her sharply across the face.

'I can't believe you have so little compassion!'

'And a fine one you are to talk!' Clare sobered abruptly, with a ruthless effort of will. 'Our whole life has been a memorial to that woman. Our marriage was only one of convenience, and I loved you so desperately. I thought I could make it work. I thought I could take on a baby and make her my own. But she turned out to be the image of her mother, even to the wine-coloured hair and violet eyes. Our marriage was cursed.'

Paddy's sky-blue eyes flashed dangerously. 'It should have worked, Clare, if your heart had been big enough. Other women take other women's children to their maternal hearts. You may recall that your friend Janet idolises her mother, her *stepmother*, that is.'

'Most women don't have to contend with obsession!' Clare screeched. 'You've never had that woman out of your mind. How *could* you, with her daughter in front of you?'

'Why don't you two stop it?' said Kit in a careful voice. 'You've had years to come to terms with the circumstances of your marriage. Today I've just learned that my parents aren't my parents at all. That you've forced me, *all* of us, to live a lie. Doesn't every thinking person know it's best to tell a child the truth? Do you think I wouldn't have accepted the fact that my real mother had died? A little child accepts what loving adults tell them. Only you never did love me, Clare, did you? Now that I think about it, you wouldn't even hold me. What a mean, hurtful woman you are! You, who have always criticised me for *my* distressing characteristics. I could never be mean to a child. Any child. I love children. I'd do anything for a child placed into my care. You can plead your excuses all you like, but at the root of it is lack of heart.'

'Indeed?' Clare laughed bitterly. 'Your father's famous for it. He deprived the Eliots of their only grandchild. He carried you off and hid you in the rain-forest. He told no one about you.'

'I was terrified they'd take you from me,' Paddy defended himself. 'They were—are—powerful people. They would have had me at their mercy. I lost Christine, I couldn't have borne to lose you. I was going out of my mind!'

'But what about my mother?' moaned Kit, trying to shut the lid on her shocking internal conflicts. 'Where was my mother all this time? Did she die in childbirth? Didn't she love me?''

'Your *mother*,' Clare said cruelly, 'that paragon of virtue, that darling of society, was married to a very influential man. He was much older, and he left her alone a lot. Your father, believe it or not, was only called to survey their country property. Your mother, apparently, took him immediately to her heart.'

'You mean, I'm illegitimate?'

'Oh, Kit darling, what on earth does that matter?' Paddy attempted to take his daughter in his arms. 'I never intended to fall in love with your mother; she never intended to fall in love with me. When you understand love, you'll know how it happened. We were swept up in a mad passion. She wasn't an ordinary woman, she came from an élite background. When she discovered she was pregnant we both went nearly crazy. I begged her to come away with me. She didn't love her husband; it was almost an arranged match. She was too young to know what she was doing and her parents greatly approved. I'm not saying he wasn't a fine man. She cared so much about him, she was determined not to hurt his career. She wanted time to handle things discreetly. She wanted *you*. Never for a moment did she consider not having you, though she and her family were faced with a great scandal. She had you very quietly. No one ever knew, not even her own mother. It was only in the last month that she even really showed. She was a strong woman and she wasn't about to go to pieces. *I* was the one who was going to pieces. She had a nurse to care for you, a woman who would have died for her. When her husband returned from a business trip in America she planned to ask him for a divorce, but they were killed on their way home from the airport. Their car careered off the highway. I don't ask myself what might have happened—I'd go mad.'

'Funny you should mention that. I think you *are* mad.' Kit stood up so quickly that she reeled.

'Darling, please sit down again. You're in shock. Clare,' Paddy spoke sternly to his wife, 'you get Kit a cup of tea, and make it sweet.'

'Goddamn it, a cup of tea!' Kit shook her head violently as if to clear it. 'Is this a fantasy? A blue movie? I'm some pathetic love-child?'

'There's nothing pathetic about you, Kit.' Paddy wiped a tear from his face. 'There was nothing pathetic about your mother, either. She decided to get on with her life and to hell with it!'

'She sounds a real beauty!'

Clare poured the tea and thrust it towards Kit, pressing her on the shoulder. 'I guess we all should plead for-

giveness. They say to know all is to understand all,' she
added harshly. 'But I feel shame. I know my limitations.
If only you'd looked like your father!'

'Thank you, no,' Kit reacted violently. 'My *father*
leaves a lot to be desired.'

Someone called Kit's name quietly behind them. Melly.

'Go away, darling,' Clare cried in agitation. 'This is
a private discussion.'

'Nothing's private,' Melly shivered, 'because Kit's *my
sister*.'

'How long have you been standing there, Melly?' Kit
moved towards the younger girl, and as she did so Melly
flung herself into her sister's arms, bursting into racking
sobs.

'*You* started this.' Paddy said angrily.

'You mean that man Stratton.' Clare looked absolutely ghastly. '*He* brought that woman here. He doesn't
like what you've done to your daughter. He's deliberately set out to be Kit's champion. He's going to rescue
her from you. He's going to return her to the bosom of
the family she should never have left.'

'Have you no pity, Clare?' Paddy asked in abject
misery.

'I had once, but it's been eroded over the years. Look
what you're doing to Melly. *She's* your daughter. Why
should Melly have to suffer?'

Paddy didn't answer, but slumped to the table, his
chin almost hitting the glossy pine.

'Give Melly to me.' Clare put our her arms.

Both girls recoiled.

'Please understand, darling,' Clare begged.

'I understand you two have been going on like a couple
of lunatics out of a movie,' Melly cried. 'Haven't you
had enough time to tell us the truth? What's the difference whether Kit's your daughter or your step-
daughter? She's *my sister*! Doesn't that say it all? I love
her, she loves me. Don't you two idiots appreciate love?'

Clare looked shocked, stretching out her hand ten-
tatively. 'It was such an extraordinary situation. Your

father found it impossible to hand over his little girl. The whole story would have had to come out. It would have been a big story. Things were different twenty years ago, a lot of people would have been hurt.'

'So you settled for hurting *me*. Thanks very much!' Kit bowed her rosy head against her sister's. 'I have to go now—I have to be by myself. Don't worry.'

'But I *do* worry.' Melly put her arms around her slender sister and hugged her to herself. 'Don't go, Kit. Stay here. We'll talk it out.'

'No, I can't talk just now.'

'Patrick, you must drive Kit to the bungalow and stay with her,' ordered Clare. 'It's simply frightful that this has happened in this way. Didn't it occur to you that one day someone would find out? What force brought Thorne Stratton up here? Damn the day!'

'You don't think it wrong to have deprived me of the truth? You don't think it wrong to deprive me of my grandparents and they of me?' demanded Kit.

'Your grandfather passed away several years ago.' Paddy lifted his head.

'Without my ever having known him.'

'I'm afraid so, my dearest girl,' Paddy said simply. 'I don't know that I'd have done things any differently. We can't be sure how your grandparents would have acted. They were devastated by the loss of their daughter. Had they known *she* had a daughter, they might have raised heaven and hell to get you. I would have been proved a scoundrel instead of the father who loves you, and I couldn't have borne an ugly court case. Your mother trusted you to me until we could work out our lives. You can be certain we would have married.'

'I'm not remotely certain about anything,' Kit said bleakly. 'My mother might well have chosen to abandon me entirely—I could have ruined her élite life.'

'What would *you* have done, Kit?' Paddy challenged her.

'I would have handled it.'

'Your *mother* was handling it.' He stared at her with tears in his eyes. 'Passion smashes lives. I believe we were victims. We might never have met, but we did. Your mother was afraid of nothing in life. She hated hurting people, but there wasn't anything she wasn't going to do to bring us all together.'

'What she did was very wrong,' said Kit urgently.

'Don't judge her, Kit,' he said gently.

Kit's brilliant eyes filled. 'My grandmother *knows* me—do you realise that?'

Paddy's blue eyes were dark with pain. 'How could she *not* know you? You were the image of your mother when you were five minutes old. You look like her, you walk like her, you talk like her—you move your hands and your head in the same way. You have the same competence. She was running two mansions when she was twenty. She didn't need help. She was swift and clever and beautiful.'

'And she married a man she didn't love?'

'She thought she loved him, my darling. He was a man with a splendid name. It was expected she would marry well. You have to be born to that life to know it, and your mother was. I was a nothing, a nobody, compared to her. I had little or no money at the time, but I was *good*. I had prospects. I could never have given her what she was used to, but I could have provided plenty of love and a comfortable home.'

'Instead of which, he got me.' Clare faced her husband, cool grey eyes burning. 'Is it any wonder I've felt cheated?'

'You shouldn't, Clare,' Patrick shook his fair, tousled head. 'I've given you everything I had.'

'Everything you had *left*!'

'It was enough to make a good life. I care for you deeply. You're always hammering away with your jealousy, but you know, whatever you think, one can't be jealous of a ghost. My love for Christine was tremendous, this side of madness. But one can't share one's life with a dead woman. I wanted to love you, but you wanted to bring the past to bed. Maybe a psychiatrist could have treated you. Or someone could have talked sense. One way and another, everything got out of hand. Kit was your whipping boy.'

'That's sick!' Melly exclaimed wrathfully. 'How could anyone take it out on a helpless little kid?'

'I did try. Don't you see?' Clare addressed her daughter emotionally. 'We had good times, of course we did. I mightn't be Kit's natural mother, but I did the best I could. I was never cruel to her—that would have been unthinkable. The real trouble was that faraway look your father gets in his eyes. Can you understand *my* feelings of helplessness and rage?'

'No, I can't,' Melly said bluntly. 'Some people enjoy suffering.'

'Melly, that's enough!' Patrick started up. 'Do you want us both to fall down on our knees?'

'It would do for a start.'

'*Please*, Melly.' Kit held up one slender, pink-tipped hand. 'Don't deprive your mother and father of their dignity. I have to be alone with my thoughts now. I love you—I'll always love you. Remember that.'

'If you think I'm going to let you go off by your-self——' Melly cried explosively.

'I'd never do anything silly, pet.' Kit's glance was shining, but very clear. She pressed her sister to her and kissed her. 'I just need to think a while.'

'Kit?'

'Yes, I do.' Kit smoothed her sister's long golden hair. 'You're not to worry about me. This is a truly incredible story, but I can handle it. After all, *I've* done nothing wrong. The people around me might have, but not me. I might go up and talk to that wonderful old lady who happens to be my grandmother. At least I can help her deal with her anguish. I knew the moment I laid eyes on her that there was a powerful link between us. Thorne must have realised it almost immediately. He was struck by my appearance that very first day.'

'He had no more idea who you were than anyone else.'
Paddy looked up at his daughter in searching wonder.
'Not then. But he's a professional. He wouldn't let up.'

'And you wouldn't talk to him?' Kit threw her father
a look of intense reproach.

'He certainly did enough talking to me.' Patrick's
mobile mouth twisted. 'He told me I would have to
answer for my crimes.'

'*Crimes?*' she echoed.

'Well, he didn't put it quite like that, but close. He
was determined to see justice done. He thinks the world
of you, Kit. He thinks you deserve every advantage.
Lately, he's been throwing in your grandmother—her
rights. He's been trying to convince me I ought to go to
her and tell her the whole story. He thought it very, very
important to tell the whole truth, but I couldn't. Not
that it helped my cause at all. I'm going to lose you
now.'

Kit walked until she was exhausted; one foot in front of
the other. What had lain dormant, deepest in her heart,
had been confirmed. She *was* a changeling, a nameless
creature, so to speak.

Am I! she thought violently. I'm *me*.

When she rode with desperate recklessness through the
double gates of the bungalow, Thorne was waiting for
her on the front porch. He took one look at the impetu-
osity of her approach and bounded down the stairs
towards her.

'Gently, Christy. Easy does it.' He grasped hold of the
handlebars of the bicycle, considerably slowing its momentum and almost dragging her off. 'Do you *have* to
go at things at that half-crazy rate?'

'Why not?' She gave a throbbing little laugh and
leaned her head back against his shoulder.

'What's up? What's the matter?' Thorne's tone was
fierce and tender both.

'Do you consider being illegitimate a tragedy or a mere
trifle?'

'My God!' He caught her deftly as she reeled, swinging her up into his arms.

'You told me to go and talk to Paddy, but Clare got in first,' she told him bitterly.

'You don't have to play tough with me, Christy,' he said urgently, sweeping her even higher. 'You're in shock.'

'Why, if you say so, Thorne, of course I am. Don't they say there's nothing worse than a woman's vengeance?'

He looked down at her briefly, his eyes flashing gold. 'Let go of the bitterness, Christy. You don't need it.'

'No, I don't,' she said in a reasonable, accommodating voice. 'I have *you*, the great Thorne Stratton. Correspondent extraordinaire, brilliant photographer, born novelist—the sky's the limit!' She laughed as though she had said something very funny.

'I'll get you into the house,' he said. 'Where's the key?'

'Come off it! I can't tell you where the key is.'

'I can't rock you on the porch.'

'Why do you bother with me at all?' she sighed.

'Because you're very important to me, Christy,' he returned curtly. 'So quit playing games. Where's the key?'

'In the pot plant.' She reached out a trembling hand in the general direction. She thought she had been coping marvellously; now, as he had so quickly diagnosed, she was being buffeted by a tidal wave of shock.

'I've got it.' With smooth economy he found the key, inserted it in the lock, opened up the door and let them in.

'How kind of you, Thorne. If it wouldn't inconvenience you, you could put me down on the couch,' Kit said.

'Do you have any spirits in the house? Brandy?'

'I certainly do,' she said frivolously. 'I'm a closet alcoholic.'

'Christy?' He seemed to be pale beneath his golden tan.

'There's some in that carved cabinet. It belongs to the owners, you know.'

'They won't mind.'

She pushed her head back on the arm of the sofa so her long curling hair fell over the other side. She kicked off her flat sandals so they wouldn't mark the lively chintz of the upholstery, the wrap-around skirt that matched her swimsuit falling back to reveal the full length of one slender golden leg.

'Ply the girl with liquor!' she ordered.

'Here, drink this,' said Thorne. 'Medicinal purposes only.'

'Aren't you going to join me?' she cried, swinging the crystal tumbler in a wild arc.

'Here, Christy...' He put his hand over hers, guiding the glass to her mouth.

'Cheers,' she choked. 'This is like poison.'

'For once, you need it.' He watched her for a moment. 'Of course, it wouldn't be like you to sip.'

'Evidently I've never heard discretion is the better part of valour. I just keep charging in.'

'Lie quiet for a minute or two. You've lost all your lovely colour.'

'I'm not surprised,' she shrugged. 'I've just had my whole life torn apart. What a story!'

'The truth *is* stranger than fiction, Christy,' said Thorne gently. 'I've covered some incredible stories.'

'You certainly made a study of mine!'

His chiselled mouth twisted. 'I figured you'd say something like that.' He shifted her legs a little so he could sit down beside her. 'Would you rather have *not* known?'

'Too late.' She put her hands over her eyes.

'Christy?' He drew her hands away, staring into her huge, tormented eyes, indigo in her pale gold face.

'Have you ever heard anything so scandalous? Neither of them let anything stand in their way, certainly not marriage vows. I'm shocked. In fact, I honestly can't find a good side to this at all. My mother betrayed her husband, her family. She betrayed *me*. I wasn't very old. I really couldn't cope by myself. How old was I when she was killed, zero plus a couple of weeks? And what about Paddy? Delightful, witty, wonderfully gregarious Paddy? He's supposed to be surveying the garden, and he's inside the house making love to the wife. "On my word of honour, I loved her!" Is that supposed to make things *right*?'

Thorne caught her frenzied hands and held them together. 'I can understand your response, Christy,' he said intensely. 'Moral judgements rest on certain standards. We're all supposed to do things according to the rules, but somehow we don't. Not one of us can't fall by the wayside at some time. Most of our lives we make a great effort to put duty and honour first, then out of nowhere we can be plunged headlong into a passionate affair. When it happens, we realise with terror that we're caught—victims, if you like. Passion is the stuff of crisis. It has powerful biological consequences. Every kind of prohibition can be swept aside. Human passion has changed history. Humans themselves differ in their degree of sexuality. Take yourself and Melly, for example. Both of you are beautiful girls, both young and innocent. It doesn't take half an experienced eye to gauge the sexuality in each of you. Any man could see at a glance that you would be far more passionate of the two. Far more likely to do something critical for love's sake. You think yourself in love with me. You would give yourself to me, I know. If I obeyed my natural impulses—powerful natural impulses, as a matter of interest—I could monopolise your life. I'm old enough and experienced enough to take a whole slice out of your life. But my feeling for you, sensual as it is, I can't deny it, has an almost sacred quality to it. I *can't* break the rules with you. I even feel I have a responsibility to ensure that you're returned to your own world. Patrick has had you all this time, but you've only been playing at life. You told me once that you never had the feeling of knowing who you *were*. In the light of what you've just found out, you can't be surprised. You have to find yourself, Christy, and you won't do that remaining here. It's no complete break from the father and sister you love, but you've been over-constricted in every possible way, cut off from the mainstream of society. Minding a store doesn't reflect your abilities—running the gallery and showcasing other people's talents. You have a very real gift of your own, a gift that deserves to be recognised. You're very articulate and intelligent, but don't you see yourself continuing your education?'

'And what am I to call myself in this brilliant world I'm about to enter?' she asked.

'Your own name obviously.'

'The whole thing's ghastly.' Kit began to rub at her temple as though she had a headache, though gradually her colour had begun to return. 'So I'm to forgive them, am I?'

'The more distant from the centre, the more censorious we tend to become. I believe Patrick when he says your mother and he struggled to the limit against their passionate attraction.'

'And no harm done, only *me*!'

'Everyone suffered, Christy. No one ever said such love doesn't bring chaos as well as heaven. Your father drew the conclusion that your grandparents would have taken you from him. They had a score to settle, and they might have been so angry and devastated that such a reaction would have been normal enough. Patrick picked you up and ran. He cloistered you up here in one of the most beautiful and isolated places in the world—or it *was*. Now that's changing. The tourists have descended on paradise. The world is too small.'

Kit nodded and turned her head. 'When did you first suspect I had a connection with the Eliots?' she asked.

'The moment I set eyes on you, your colouring was familiar, then the bone structure. There's little evidence now, but Lady Eliot had the most beautiful red hair. Moreover, if you had time to notice, her eyes are still brilliant and so blue they're almost violet. I've seen photographs of your mother as a young woman and basically, you're her double. Lady Eliot was terribly shaken. And then there's your voice and your manner. You only spoke to your grandmother very briefly, but it was enough for her to say you're of her blood. She has claimed you, Christy, without another question.'

CHAPTER NINE

IT WAS a measure of Lady Eliot's love that Kit's twenty-first birthday party was planned as a great celebration. The cream of society were invited; some four hundred guests.

On that brilliant blue morning, the vast harbourside mansion, almost baronial in style, bustled with activity. An army of gardeners combed the magnificent grounds. Two gigantic pink and white marquees were set up on the lawn, and dozens of pink and blue water-lilies were made to swim in the pool. Vans kept arriving, and masses and masses of flowers filled the huge rooms. Lady Eliot had remembered everybody. It seemed to her that she had never been happier, when only twelve short months before she had thought she had little left to live for. The untrammelled happiness she had been searching for all her life was finally in her grasp; her beloved grand-daughter had been restored to her. Now, as she looked out over the bustling activity in the garden, the tears of joy came to her. In these past twelve months, the sun shone more brightly than it had ever done before. The blue waters of the harbour looked deeper, richer, more dazzling. The air had a special clarity and fresh tang. The traumatic days were over, for Lady Eliot had always carried deep in her heart terrible doubts about the last turbulent year of her daughter's life. Christine had been very rich and very beautiful, but her passionate nature had led to her own destruction. If only she had seen more of her daughter—but her husband's diplomatic posting had kept them in Paris for most of the time. It was a disturbing story, but the tragic consequences had been swept away as Christy became central to Lady Eliot's life.

Christy was such a dear girl, so vivid, yet so steady. She had inherited all her mother's fabled beauty, but it seemed to Lady Eliot that Christy carried within her the best of all their characteristics. Many of their friends, dazzled by Christy's warmth and beauty, insisted she was very much like Lady Eliot herself. No family, no matter how exalted, was entirely free of scandal. A rich source of gossip at the beginning, Christy had triumphed on the social scene, not only because of her grandmother's entrenched position, but because of her own friendly and confident personality.

Lady Eliot was so proud of her. The intensity of her devotion shone out of her eyes. It had been the greatest joy to introduce her granddaughter to society and take her on a whirlwind trip to the United Kingdom and the great cities of Europe. Their shared experiences were unforgettable. Never a night passed that Lady Eliot didn't thank God on her knees for the last and greatest gift of all, her beloved granddaughter. Whatever forces had been prevalent in Christy's childhood—and Lady Eliot had her own view of Clare Lacey—Christy's essential strength of character had allowed her to cope. Now, as an adult, she had such a warm elegance of manner that she drew everyone to her, and the cultural experiences she had gained on their travels were showing in the scope of her work. Christy's ability as an artist was quite a topic of discussion, and Lady Eliot was delighted to see her working so hard. Life without commitment was meaningless, and Christy was no social butterfly. Her talent and her sense of responsibility to it set her apart.

Always, when Lady Eliot thought of her granddaughter, her thoughts came around to Thorne Stratton. Both of them owed him everything. Thorne had returned her granddaughter to her, almost in the process renouncing her himself. But Lady Eliot knew well the direction of her granddaughter's heart's desire. Not that there was an outward expression of it; they might have been caring cousins. Christy deferring sweetly all the while to Thorne's superior wisdom. Or so it seemed.

Underneath lurked the danger zone. It existed simultaneously with the easy camaraderie. They met often, though not lately, as Thorne had been in London for months, being fêted by his publishers. It was claimed in the Press that he had been offered an all-time high advance for a first novel, but his publishers were so confident of the manuscript of *The Last Dawn* that they were mounting a large-scale promotion. Thorne had found a new career for himself as a potential best-selling author, and he told anyone who asked that he owed his success in some degree to Christy. It was she who had challenged him to turn his experiences against the background of South-East Asia into a compelling story. And thus it was. Even film rights were being discussed.

No one was at all sure he would be able to return to Sydney in time for Christy's birthday party. Success *was* seductive, and all his family were around him to share in his triumph, but a call had come through last night to say he was in the last stages of his flight from London. He would be arriving from Singapore mid-morning.

Outwardly so composed, Christy had betrayed the inner disappointment she had been carrying with an absolute radiance. Her laughter and excitement carried them through the almost manic activity associated with the last-minute preparations for large parties. The scene was set for a truly glittering occasion. Even Lady Eliot's attitude towards Patrick Lacey had changed. Her love for Christy had compelled her to forgive him—and then, Christy was so fond of her sister. They had seen a lot of Melanie during the past year. She was the flower to Christy's flame. Christy had insisted on hanging her father's portrait of the two girls, and Lady Eliot had to admit it *was* lovely.

Kit was putting the final touches to her springing mane when Lady Eliot knocked on her bedroom door. Kit hurried to it, knowing it was her grandmother and anticipating her reaction by going into a sweeping curtsy. She looked up laughingly and Lady Eliot held out a shaking hand.

'My darling, you look glorious! Every other word fails.' As enchanted as she was, Christy's startling resemblance to her mother momentarily upset Lady Eliot, and she had to bite her lip hard.

'Nanna, you have tears in your eyes, and you *can't* have tears in your eyes on such a wonderful night! Look at me.'

'I'm looking,' Lady Eliot smiled.

'I could write a book about loving and being loved,' Christy told her. 'This last year has been the happiest of my life, the most fulfilling, the most contented. And all because of you. I never have to explain myself to you. You know my every thought, my every move. We're *that* close!'

'Indeed we are, my darling.' Lady Eliot briskly blinked her lids. 'Now stand back so I can get a proper look at you.'

Kit did as she was told, swaying the marvellous ball-skirt of her long, romantic gown. The material was a wonderfully lustrous duchesse satin with a net under-skirt. The tight-fitting bodice was strapless, dipping gently to a delicately shadowed cleft. The tiny waist was marked by a big, beautifully tied centre bow and the colour was gardenia. Against its rich lustre, Kit's skin and dark crimson hair shimmered and glowed.

Lady Eliot had to discipline herself not to burst into tears. She was so romantic and sentimental, and Christy looked like a painting come to life. 'Lovely, my darling,' she said huskily. 'You only need a little jewellery to set off the splendour of your gown. Come to my room for a moment.'

'After I admire *you*.' Kit swished eagerly around her grandmother's spare and graceful frame. Lady Eliot was wearing her favourite shade of blue, a deep hyacinth, and her magnificent pearls, her husband's wedding gift to her almost fifty years ago. Their value had increased phenomenally, and one day they would Christy's. The matching jacket of her long gown featured sequined and beaded roses, and she wore diamond earclips to match the exquisite clasp on her pearls which she nearly always turned to one side.

'If I've learnt anything about the art of dressing over the past twelve months, it's from you,' Kit exclaimed with admiration in her eyes.

'My darling girl, you really have tremendous style of your own. I won't protest if you say it's inherited. Actually, my hair was just your colour. I expect when you're an old lady like me your hair will be snow-white. It never streaked grey, it simply went white. Now, come along and see what I've got for you. I'm longing to see your reaction. You might like to make a final check on everything before the guests arrive. Edith is marvellous, but she's not as young as she used to be. Besides, she's so excited, she's almost mad!'

When Kit descended the grand staircase, everyone clapped.

The entrance hall was a dazzle of black and white marble, of great Chinese porcelain jars filled with flowers and a sea of smiling, upturned faces illuminated by the dripping jewels of the great overhead chandelier.

Patrick and Clare were there—Clare very elegant in ivory lace and as composed as ever, Paddy all golden beard and blue eyes and looking visibly perturbed. There was Melly, looking ravishing in blue and silver chiffon, clinging to Glenn's hand, all the beautiful people Kit had met, the handsome eligible young men who had been introduced into her life and whose company she had enjoyed without coming within light years of losing her heart. Only one man set her alight. Only one man took hold of her mind, and *he* was leaning against an Italian rococo gilt console, looking so stunningly handsome he made every other man look staid beside him.

Kit felt the shock-waves break around her. There was an almost mystical intensity about her feeling for him: an endless secret yearning. Her violet eyes smouldered, and without quite realising what she was doing she threw him a look that was close to a challenge. There was something dangerous about his leonine splendour, the dazzle of light making his thick, longish hair glint softly metallic. Sensation spun in her brain.

'To our evening's star, my granddaughter!' Lady Eliot announced proudly.

For an instant, Kit was robbed of the power of movement. She wore a necklace of platinum, diamond flowers and sapphires around her throat and matching sapphire and diamond clips at her ears, yet even the brilliance of the jewels was only a decoration.

Thorne, she thought. *Thorne*. Desire was like musk in her mouth.

It took a long time to get through the receiving line. Thorne kissed her on the forehead, then briefly on her full, tender lips. The sensation was extreme, the excitement astounding, but such was the completeness of Kit's education that she smiled up at him as though she was entirely used to men fighting for her attention. The truly enjoyable part was that such *had* happened. Many a young man over the past year had become lost in admiration.

The old white and gold ballroom had been opened up again for this grand occasion. The opulent plasterwork had been picked out again in gold and the walls had been repainted an eggshell blue. The springing polished floor was perfect, and almost an entire symphony orchestra had been set up on the raised stage. When one of Kit's most persistent admirers, a young up-and-coming QC called Roger Westcott, swirled her confidently into the mainstream of dancers, they were playing a Billy Joel favourite, the pianist making much of the recently retuned Steinway concert grand.

Roger held her close to him, murmuring the lyrics quite tunefully in her ear, altering them slightly to suit himself:

'You're such a temptation,
You're driving me crazy,
And it's my fascination
That makes me act this way...'

His hand ran with a certain possessiveness along her bare skin. 'Why don't we do something exciting tomorrow? You don't have to stay home, do you? Because, if you do, I'll come over and help you open the presents. My God, where are you ever going to find the space to store them? There are some fabulous things there.'

Kit closed her eyes briefly. Across the huge, beautiful room, adorned with the women's dresses in all the colours of the rainbow, Thorne was being lionised. It gave her an odd feeling of melancholy, so much so that to combat it she gave Roger more encouragement than he had received all year. She could feel the excitement and tension building in her. The party had been in progress almost an hour, yet apart from those first few minutes Thorne had had little to say to her. At least he hadn't brought one of his usual glamorous companions.

'What did you say, Roger?' Kit asked.

'Nothing important.' He held her away from him. 'No one looks like you. No one has your style. Yet I find you so elusive. As soon as I get close to you, you back away.'

Roger was not allowed to monopolise the birthday girl. Kit was in ceaseless demand, unaware for the most part that Thorne's amber glance pinned her wherever she was. She looked astonishingly beautiful and gloriously flirtatious, her gaiety so obvious it made other people want to bask in it.

Patrick claimed her the moment her latest partner went off to fetch her a long, frosty drink.

'You want to dance with your old father?'

'Of course I do, Paddy. You know I love you.'

'Yes,' Patrick said in a wondering tone. 'You've judged me very kindly.'

'I don't judge you at all, Paddy.' Kit smiled up at her father with love and compassion in her eyes. 'What you did was for me. You knew I could never be happy without you and you thought my grandparents would take me away. It's all in the past, Paddy. We must put it behind us. The future is all that matters. Things are easier for you with Clare?'

'Clare tries—we've both been trying very hard. I asked too much of her. She couldn't play my game. *You're* happy, aren't you?'

'Wonderfully happy.' Her violet eyes deepened. 'Knowing who I am has given me a reality. Do you know what I mean?'

'Of course I do.' Patrick dropped a kiss on the top of his daughter's head. 'We all need to make sense of ourselves. I'm even pushing further afield with my own artistic efforts. Do you remember when you said I had a special gift for portraiture?'

'Yes, Paddy?' Kit was so interested, she stopped dancing.

'Well,' Paddy grinned, 'I've been offered a few commissions. Believe it or not, Peter Leighton wants a portrait of his new wife. Pity he didn't ask me before—he could have had a gallery.'

'I'm thrilled for you, Paddy,' Kit told him with infinite pleasure. 'It doesn't hurt, either, to have such a rich man for a patron.'

'Especially one who makes a habit of getting divorced and remarrying. Can you see the women lost in admiration around Thorne?'

'No, where?' Kit lied.

'Still in love with him, darlin'?'

'Correction, Paddy. Not *in love*. What I feel for Thorne I'll carry all my life—no easy thing.'

'Well, he's certainly a first-rate human being, and we needed him. I wasn't glad at the time, but I am now. Mountains can be moved with understanding and love. I think your grandmother has forgiven me?'

'You know she has, Paddy. She told me she never, ever thought to spend such a happy year. And we have the years to come. We're *family*, Paddy, and Nanna is very fond of Melly.'

'You know she and Glenn have been seeing a great deal of each other?'

'She told me. She's very young, but she seems to know her own heart and mind.'

'The blindfold is off his eyes,' said Paddy. 'He realised you were the impossible dream. Even Mrs Cowley isn't a problem. She already treats Melly like a daughter.'

'Well, we'll see,' Kit smiled slightly. 'Melly has a pretty good time here. She'll come to marriage when she's ready.'

The buffet supper was sumptuous, the long white damask-covered tables groaning with the unrivalled food resources of the country—and the USSR as well, for there was plenty of caviar. The speeches were short and witty. Lady Eliot's brought the sparkle of tears; Thorne's delighted applause. Kit responded sweetly, with all her heart. Afterwards, the ladies retired in perfumed waves to repair their make-up and indulge in a little private gossip, while the party went on with renewed vivacity.

'Wait for me here,' a sexy voice whispered in Kit's ear: Roger. He smiled at her, then walked inside briskly to secure champagne. Kit had never danced so much in her life. Now she sought a brief respite. She looked around quickly for an empty chair, but as she moved towards one Thorne materialised out of nowhere and grasped her arm.

'You've danced enough!' He drew her out on to the long, colonnaded terrace where couples strolled arm in arm.

'Really?' Kit gave him a sidelong, upward glance. 'From anyone else but you, I would have said your nose was out of joint.'

'You *do* want to escape Roger, don't you?'

'But he's charming!' she smiled.

'Sure. That's why you've been daydreaming as he spins you around in his arms.'

'*Now* where are we going?' asked Kit.

They were moving towards the arched loggia on the north side which led to the sub-tropical extravagance of the conservatory.

'It's customary to seek a quiet corner when one wants to be alone,' Thorne told her.

'I don't understand, Thorne. You want to be alone with *me*?'

'Isn't that what you've been thinking about?'

'I'm sure all the adulation you've been receiving has turned your head.'

'Why won't you look at me?' he asked softly.

'I'm not sure I want to.' Kit bent her head so that her ruby-coloured hair fell around her in a curtain. 'It can't have been easy for you, coming home for my party.'

'My dear Christy, nothing would have made me miss it.'

Her neck arched and she averted her lovely profile. 'All the ladies have been falling upon you ecstatically—the literary lion in our midst. We're very proud of you, Thorne.'

'And to think I did it all for you!' he said drily.

'Well, you *have* been telling people I put the idea into your head.'

'That, for a start. You look extraordinarily beautiful tonight, yet I can still picture you that first day on the beach.'

'I don't intend to sunbathe topless again,' Kit assured him.

'I think you will.' There was a sardonic inflection in his voice. 'On your honeymoon. Some secluded beach where your husband can delight in your beautiful body.'

She assumed a mock severity. 'I don't intend to get married for years yet.'

'Can it be you no longer love me?'

Kit turned her head towards him, tilting her chin. 'You were the one who convinced me that loving you wasn't right.'

Thorne laughed abruptly. 'My God, that was a year ago!'

'You've obviously been counting the days,' she responded in a bitter-sweet voice. 'I think I prefer you as an absolute dear. *Cousin Thorne.*'

'Lady Eliot tells me Westcott is in love with you,' Thorne remarked. '*Is* he?'

'Of course. What's actually wrong with that? It may surprise you to know that I've enjoyed considerable popularity among the socially ambitious. I've even thrown off my attachment to *you*.'

'You mean, it's been necessary for *me* to backtrack while *you've* been developing? We're bound together, Christy, by a powerful force. You've done a lot of things in the past year, and I've had to allow you to. The question I asked at the beginning is, do you still love me?'

'*No!*' she said in a little frantic outburst. 'I just don't happen to like what you've done to me this year.'

'Shall we clear that up?' Thorne's eyes travelled with searing deliberation over her flushed face, lingering on the tell-tale rise and fall of her breasts. There was a burnished flame at the centre.

'Don't you attempt to touch me,' whispered Kit defensively.

'Would you prefer it to be someone else?' His mouth curved ironically.

'At least then I could be sure of the outcome!'

'You do have the reputation of being something of an ice-maiden.' Behind the mockery was a conflicting steely thread of approval.

'But you know differently, don't you?' She tossed her ruby head, her hair swinging in a heavy, scented arc away from the long slender column of her neck. '*You* have a power over me nobody else does. Self-control seems to flee me when you're around.'

'And what does that mean?' His beautiful, patrician voice had an amused, upward inflection.

'As far as I'm concerned,' she confirmed sharply, 'Thorne spells out D-a-n-g-e-r.'

'And just what kind of madness did you have in mind?'

She shrugged her sloping bare shoulders. 'Excuse me, I have nothing in mind!'

'Well, *I* have!' There was a matchless male arrogance in his voice.

Kit wasn't feigning her shock. 'Thorne, there are four hundred people all around us!' she reminded him.

'I'm well aware of that,' he said drily. 'I'm only going to kiss you. *Only*, dear God!'

'Don't do this to me, Thorne,' she threatened, trying unsuccessfully to retreat.

'How can I not? Come here to me, Christy.' He lifted his hand and caressed her in a gesture as tender as it was erotic. 'When have I ever hurt you? Your well-being has always been uppermost in my mind. I've denied myself you for a whole year. I don't deserve protests, I deserve praise. What do you think I'm made of, anyway—clay? You'd turn bronze molten. There hasn't been a single night in this past year that I haven't had you invade my dreams. I've imagined you endlessly beside me. It was the only way I could keep going.'

'I don't believe this!' Kit shook her head. 'You've never even touched me, never so much as taken my arm.'

'And we both know why! An alcoholic doesn't have the occasional drink. I was sworn off.'

'It was cruel,' she whispered.

'It served its purpose.' His arm moved out to imprison her. 'It was hell to wait, but I always intended to claim you.'

His admission was breathtaking. 'Just like that?' Kit's eyes glittered as her quick temper rose.

'It's always been my plan.' Thorne's eyes rested with supreme confidence on her mutinous face.

'And, just like a general, you didn't consider letting me know?'

'Hush, Christy!' He swirled her further down the loggia, where they merged with the patterned shadows. The leaves of the trees whispered all around them. The moon rose brilliantly over the walled rose garden that gave off a glorious night-time perfume.

'I had to allow you to establish other relationships,' he pointed out with harsh intensity. 'In fact, I've learnt a truly Oriental patience. But I had no doubt of the outcome. At this point, I don't like to consider what I would have done had you turned to someone else. Maybe there's a facet of my personality *I* don't want to go into I've avoided saying it, but before God I mean it. You're mine, Christy. My woman. Maybe every man passionately in love is a throwback to primitive times. I want you quite desperately—your whole life. And I *will* have it!'

Kit was so keyed up, she even welcomed his aggressiveness. 'Barbarian!' she blazed.

'*Am* I?''

His mastery, the fierce possessiveness of it, pierced her heart. From hostility, she was instantly open and vulnerable. As his mouth came down passionately to enclose hers, it flowered like a rose.

The old familiar ecstasy! Thorne was crushing her to his tall lean body, the strength of his emotion betrayed by the fine tremor in his strong arms.

'I missed you...' she breathed into his mouth. ' couldn't bear it...all I offered you, you didn't want...

'Little fool!' His vibrant, impeccable voice was faintly slurred.

Heat radiated all over Kit's body. She was shuddering against him. If only she were free of her clothes! She wanted him with a passion that confounded her. It was a kind of anguish to keep to this fiery kissing.

'*God*, Christy!' he echoed her intense frustration.

She moved her mouth around his beloved face, her nostrils drinking in his male scent.

'Tell me you love me,' he muttered.

'Utterly.' She kissed the side of his mouth. 'I need to show you. So much!' The pulse that beat so hectically in her vulnerable throat showed her longing.

'My beautiful girl!' His mouth claimed hers again with power and abandonment, so that for some moments they were astonishingly mindless of time and place. The earth really did fade, as an unrelenting excitement transported them upwards into a cloud world. The bubbles in their blood were celestial jewels, brilliant and fiery.

It was Thorne who broke their impassioned embrace, though from the taut expression on his handsome face he found the effort almost intolerable.

'I don't know exactly when we'll be married,' he said huskily. 'I expect Lady Eliot will want a say in it, but we're getting engaged right away.' With his strong left arm still locked around her, he reached into the inner breast pocket of his dinner-jacket and drew out a small, glittering object that made her gasp.

'*Thorne!*'

'I'm here,' he said gently, indulgent of her reaction. 'Could I have your hand, do you think?'

Kit lifted her left hand bemusedly, and he turned it palm up and kissed it. 'What other stone could I choose but a sapphire, with your eyes?' He slipped the ring over her long slender finger, the diamonds that surrounded the exquisite central jewel glittering as they reflected the beam of strong moonlight.

'It's beautiful...so beautiful...' The tears sprang to her eyes.

'The colour of heaven. Like your eyes.' Thorne took her rapt face between his strong hands and kissed her wet eyelids, then her quivering mouth.

'Whatever I expected, I never expected *this*!' she told him.

'I don't see why not, my darling,' he said reasonably. 'Your grandmother is all set to announce our engagement.'

'Are you serious?' Her eyes were huge.

'I've never been more serious in my life.' The humour disappeared, to be replaced by an unforgettable serious-ness and passion. 'You're my life, Christiana. From this moment onwards, I am yours. I give you my solemn oath that I will never hurt or betray you. I offer you all my love, my support, my protection. I'll never let you go—you *must* understand that. You're still so young. You're a very beautiful woman and your beauty will grow. I'm not the first man or the last man to love you, but I'm the only man in your life. If you ever disregard that, then you would find me dangerous. You are the one and only woman I want. I will have little sympathy for anyone who tries to come between us.'

He sounded so severe, so...ruthless, Kit looked up at him for reassurance. 'Why are you talking to me like this?' she begged.

'A warning, my darling.' He pushed back the heavy hair from her face. 'Only one. I never want you to forget it.'

In one instant of understanding, she saw all the pain of his childhood, the havoc his beautiful mother's 'defection' had wrought.

'You're not the only one who can make sacred vows,' she told him with loving intensity. 'Do you know, I thank God on my knees every night for the great love he has brought me? You must know my true nature, or why else would you love me? Fidelity is my great strength. Put your old fears to rest, my beloved. I'm a one-man woman!'

She looked so fabulously beautiful and positive, Thorne swept her into his arms.

So much love. So much life. Waiting for both of them.

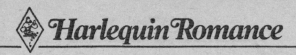 **Harlequin Romance**

Coming Next Month

2941 WHIRLPOOL OF PASSION Emma Darcy
Ashley finds Cairo fascinating, and even more so the mysterious sheikh she encounters in the casino. She's aware their attraction is mutual, but doesn't take it seriously until he kidnaps her....

2942 THIS TIME ROUND Catherine George
It's all very well for Leo Seymour to want to share her life, Davina thinks, but she can't forget that his first love married her brother years ago. Would Davina's secret love for him be enough to sustain their relationship?

2943 TO TAME A TYCOON Emma Goldrick
It isn't that Laura absolutely doesn't trust tycoon Robert Carlton; she only wants to protect her young daughter from him. And Robert has all his facts wrong about Laura. If there was only some way to change their minds about each other.

2944 AT FIRST SIGHT Eva Rutland
From the time designer Cicely Roberts accidentally meets psychiatrist-author Mark Dolan, her life is turned upside down. Even problems she didn't know she had get straightened out—and love comes to Cicely at last!

2945 CATCH A DREAM Celia Scott
Jess is used to rescuing her hapless cousin Kitty from trouble, but confronting Andros Kalimantis in his lonely tower in Greece is the toughest thing she's ever done. And Kitty hadn't warned her that Andros is a millionaire....

2946 A NOT-SO-PERFECT MARRIAGE Edwina Shore
James's suspected unfaithfulness was the last straw. So Roz turned to photography, left James to his business and made a successful career on her own. So why should she even consider letting him back into her life now?

Available in November wherever paperback books are sold, or through Harlequin Reader Service:

In the U.S.
901 Fuhrmann Blvd.
P.O. Box 1397
Buffalo, N.Y. 14240-1397

In Canada
P.O. Box 603
Fort Erie, Ontario
L2A 5X3

Taylor House

by Leigh Anne Williams

Enter the lives of the Taylor women of Greensdale, Massachusetts, a town where tradition and family mean so much. A story of family, home and love in a New England village.

Don't miss the Taylor House trilogy, starting next month in Harlequin American Romance with #265 *Katherine's Dream*, in October 1988, and followed by #269 *Lydia's Hope* and #273 *Clarissa's Wish* in November and December of 1988.

One house . . . two sisters . . . three generations

ATTRACTIVE, SPACE SAVING BOOK RACK

Display your most prized novels on this handsome and sturdy book rack. The hand-rubbed walnut finish will blend into your library decor with quiet elegance, providing a practical organizer for your favorite hard-or soft-covered books.

Only $9.95

Approximately 16" x 8" when assembled

Assembles in seconds!

To order, rush your name, address and zip code, along with a check or money order for $10.70* ($9.95 plus 75¢ postage and handling) payable to *Harlequin Reader Service*:

Harlequin Reader Service
Book Rack Offer
901 Fuhrmann Blvd.
P.O. Box 1396
Buffalo, NY 14269-1396

Offer not available in Canada.

BKR-1A

*New York and Iowa residents add appropriate sales tax.